JOHN MACLELLAN

Nass Valley Sasquatch

THE FORESTS OF BRITISH COLUMBIA HOLD A DARK SECRET

First published by Copper Mountain Books 2023

Copyright © 2023 by John MacLellan

All rights reserved. No part of this publication may be reproduced, stored or transmitted in any form or by any means, electronic, mechanical, photocopying, recording, scanning, or otherwise without written permission from the publisher. It is illegal to copy this book, post it to a website, or distribute it by any other means without permission.

This novel is entirely a work of fiction. The names, characters and incidents portrayed in it are the work of the author's imagination. Any resemblance to actual persons, living or dead, events or localities is entirely coincidental.

John MacLellan asserts the moral right to be identified as the author of this work.

Designations used by companies to distinguish their products are often claimed as trademarks. All brand names and product names used in this book and on its cover are trade names, service marks, trademarks and registered trademarks of their respective owners. The publishers and the book are not associated with any product or vendor mentioned in this book. None of the companies referenced within the book have endorsed the book.

This book contains real locations in and around British Columbia, Canada.

First edition

This book was professionally typeset on Reedsy. Find out more at reedsy.com

This book is dedicated to my Wife Wendy Ross-MacLellan. To my son's Jevon MacLellan, Guy Roberts and family. This is also dedicated to Thomas, Hans, Douglas, Sonya, Allison and family. All of you bring joy to my life. To all my Native friends and family members who all accept me as their Brother and Uncle. To my Brothers Wayne and James MacLellan. Also to all of my family in Nova Scotia. I love you all from the bottom of my heart. Sasquatch, you elusive bugger. You will be found some day.

Contents

Research Nass Valley	ii
Hairy man of the woods	x
Guided Tour	xiii
Grizzly Survival	xvi
Tseax Volcano	xxv
Emergency Extraction	xxxvi
The Hunter's Cabin	xlv
Camera Seven	liii
Jenny and Skyler Gather Firewood	lxii
Kidnapped By Sasquatch	lxvi
White Light In The Sky	lxxvi
Keep Our Secret	lxxxiv
Betterment of the world	xciv
The Proposal	xcviii
The Research Community	c
About the Author	2

Research Nass Valley

Dr. Lisa Ross is a Biological Anthropologist with a Ph.D. from the University of British Columbia (UBC). She is renowned for her expertise in studying human biology and evolution, particularly focusing on analyzing hominid fossils and reconstructing human evolutionary history.

She has traveled to various corners of the world, including Africa, Europe, and Asia, where she has worked on numerous field projects to uncover new insights into the evolutionary origins of modern humans. Her innovative research has been published in top-tier scientific journals and has contributed significantly to the field of biological anthropology.

Dr. Ross is flying to Northern British Columbia to do a research project North of Terrace, BC, She is to meet with Tom Miller, a local Sasquatch researcher, to embark on an exciting research expedition to the Nass Valley. The objective of the trip was to explore the possibility of a hominid species in the region, a project that Dr. Ross was eager to pursue.

With her extensive knowledge and experience in the field of biological anthropology, Dr. Ross was an invaluable asset to the team. Her leadership and expertise were instrumental in identifying potential hominid fossil sites, collecting relevant data, and analyzing the findings to provide critical insights into the evolutionary history of hominids.

Dr. Ross's work has not only shed new light on the origins of our species but has also inspired future generations of anthropologists to continue exploring and unraveling the mysteries of human evolution.

She continues to be a leading figure in the field, with her research shaping our understanding of our evolutionary past and future.

Dr. Ross was contemplating how to tell her husband, David, about her upcoming trip out of town. She knew he would not be happy, as he was a control freak and had reacted poorly the last time she had to leave for work. She considered not telling him but knew that would only be a mistake and make things worse.

As a Biological Anthropologist, Ph.D. Dr. Ross held a prestigious position at the university. However, David often belittled her work, saying things like "you took ten years to study dead things" and suggesting that "saving people is a more important job than studying dead hominids." These statements would often lead to fights between the couple.

As David entered their home and sat down to watch the news, Dr. Ross nervously sat on the couch next to him. She struggled to find the right words to tell him about her trip, but ultimately blurted out, "I have a research project up North I have to go and do." David responded with anger, reminding her of her previous promises that it would be the last time she would have to leave. She explained that there were reported sightings of a rare, ape-like creature, a Sasquatch and that she needed to go to the field to find evidence of its existence. She mentioned that she and her colleague, Jenny, would fly to Terrace the next day.

David scoffed at the idea of a "Sasquatch" and suggested that it probably did not exist. Dr. Ross, however, remained determined to uncover the truth. David thought that maybe she would be eaten by the creature and he would collect on her insurance. "I don't care, Lisa. You always have some new project that you have to run off to. I'm tired of it." He stood up and walked out of the room, leaving Dr. Ross sitting there feeling perplexed and confused. Lisa followed David into the bedroom and confronted him about his behavior. When she entered the room, she found him sitting on the edge of the bed with his head in his hands. She asked him why he always walked into the bedroom when they argued, and he told her that it was because he didn't want a replay of the last argument.

She felt a wave of relief wash over her. For once, David had not blown up in anger or broken anything in the house upon hearing about her research trip. She realized that she had been allowing his dismissive attitude toward her work to make her feel guilty about her passion for her field. This time she refused to let that happen. She made a mental note not to let his lack of understanding and support keep her from pursuing her goals any longer. She was determined to make the most of this opportunity and come back with groundbreaking findings for her research.

Dr. Ross arrived at Vancouver International Airport and made her way through the crowds to the designated meeting spot for her colleague, Jenny. As she approached, she spotted Jenny waving and smiling, her baggage cart was loaded with equipment and bags. "Lisa! Over here!" Jenny called out. Dr. Ross walked over, and they hugged each other, happy to finally embark on this research project together. Jenny is a driven and passionate 4th-year Biological Anthropologist student studying under the guidance of esteemed researcher Dr. Lisa Ross. Her dedication to the field and eagerness to explore new research areas have made her a standout student in her program.

Recently, Jenny was tasked with a unique opportunity to join Dr. Ross on an exciting research expedition to the Nass Valley to study a potential Hominid species. This was a rare opportunity for a student of her level, and Jenny was thrilled to be chosen for the project.

With her background in biological anthropology, Jenny brought a unique perspective and skills to the research team. Her enthusiasm and curiosity made her an invaluable asset, and she was eager to contribute to the project in any way she could.

During other expeditions, Jenny worked alongside Dr. Ross to identify potential hominid fossil sites, collect data, and analyze the findings. Her strong analytical skills and attention to detail were vital in this complex and challenging research project.

Through her work on this expedition, Jenny will gain invaluable hands-on experience in the field of biological anthropology. She has been given this opportunity to contribute to the discovery of a potentially ground breaking new hominid species, and her dedication and hard work have impressed her colleagues and mentors alike.

Jenny's passion for biological anthropology and her drive to contribute to the field have set her on a path toward a successful research career. Her work on this project has solidified her commitment to studying human biology and evolution, and she looks forward to continuing to explore new research areas in the future.

After checking in their baggage, the two women made their way to their gate, chatting excitedly about their upcoming journey. They boarded the flight to Terrace and settled into their seats, both feeling a mix of nerves and anticipation. Dr. Ross couldn't help but feel uneasy about David's reaction to her trip, but she pushed the thoughts out of her mind and focused on the work ahead.

As the plane landed in Terrace, Dr. Ross and Jenny collected their bags and made their way out of the airport. Waiting for them outside was Tom Miller. Tom Miller is a seasoned entrepreneur and the CEO and owner of Tom's Wood, Timber & Trucking, a leading timber company in the region. Despite his busy work schedule, Tom has an unusual and fascinating hobby – he has seen Sasquatch multiple times throughout his life.

At 60, Tom has had a lifelong fascination with the elusive creature, having first spotted it when he was a child. Although he hasn't been close to Sasquatch, his sightings have fueled his curiosity and spurred him to become an expert on the creature's habits and habitat.

Tom's expertise and knowledge of the Nass Valley region have made him a valuable contact for Dr. Lisa Ross in her research on this potential new hominid species. He provides guidance and support to Dr. Ross and Jenny, offering valuable insights into the area's unique ecology and terrain.

Beyond his knowledge of the area, Tom is also an accomplished hunter and fisherman with a deep understanding of the natural resources and wildlife in the region. He provides essential security and cooking for the team while on their research expeditions, ensuring their safety and sustenance during their time in the wilderness.

Tom's passion for the outdoors and his unusual encounters with Sasquatch have made him a fascinating figure in the region. His dedication and expertise have earned him the respect of his colleagues and community, and he remains an integral part of Dr. Ross's research team in the Nass Valley. He greeted them warmly and loaded their bags into his truck before driving them towards the Nisga'a highway.

"I've got some bad news," he said. "There's been a report of a local man from Terrace who went missing three weeks ago. He was out hunting and never returned." Tom hands the Terrace newspaper to Lisa. Lisa read the news report to Jenny while Tom listened,

"Terrace Hunter Goes Missing, Found Dead After 2-Week Search. A hunter from Terrace went missing earlier this month, sparking a widespread search effort that lasted for two weeks. Sadly, the search ended with a grisly discovery. A team member came upon a deceased man in the dense forest, later identified as the missing hunter.

According to the local police, an animal is believed to have attacked and killed the hunter, causing his death. The coroner has been notified, and an investigation is underway to determine the exact cause of death.

This tragedy serves as a reminder of the dangers of venturing into the wilderness and the importance of taking necessary precautions and being properly equipped when going on hunting trips or hikes. Our thoughts and condolences go out to the family and loved ones of the deceased hunter."

Dr. Ross felt a pit in her stomach as Tom recounted the man's death. It was a harsh reminder of the risks involved in their research. She couldn't help but think about the man's family and how they must feel.

Dr. Ross and Jenny were left to ponder the possibility that the creature they had come to study could be responsible for the man's death. It was a sobering thought, and they knew they had to be extra careful as they continued their research. They knew their work was important, but it now had a new sense of urgency.

As they drove, they stopped at the Rosswood General Store to stock up on supplies. The store was small but had everything they needed, from camping gear to food. They spent some time browsing and chatting with the store owner, who was also excited about their research and offered to help in any way he could. He told a story about when he was hunting. In the distance, he saw a large bipedal animal in the river. Then it walked out of the river, and he realized it was a Sasquatch. It was massive and tall. He was glad it was far away. But he left the forest.

After a quick lunch break, they were back on the road, eager to reach their destination and begin their research.

The Nass Valley is a remote and rugged area of British Columbia, known for its dense forests, the Lava Beds, the Tseax volcano, and towering mountain ranges. For centuries, it has been home to the Nisga'a people, who had lived in harmony with the land and its wildlife. But there was one creature that the Nisga'a had respect for: the Sasquatch, or as it was more commonly known, the hairy man of the woods.

The legend of the hairy man of the woods had been passed down through generations of Nisga'a storytellers. They spoke of a giant, ape-like creature that roamed the forest, leaving behind large footprints and an eerie howl that echoed through the valleys. Some said it was a supernatural spirit, a powerful force of nature that should be respected and feared. Others claimed it was a real animal, a missing link between apes and humans that had somehow managed to evade discovery, and some called it another kind of human.

Despite the legends, most outsiders dismissed the idea of a giant, ape-like creature roaming the wilderness as nothing more than a myth. But a small group of researchers and enthusiasts refused to give up on their quest to find the truth. They spent decades scouring the forest for evidence, interviewing locals, and analyzing every piece of information that came their way.

Navigating the Nass Valley wilderness in search of Sasquatch presented many challenges for the trio. The valley was a vast and rugged landscape covered in dense forests, deep canyons, and steep mountains. The terrain could be difficult to traverse, with steep inclines, rocky outcroppings, and a swift-moving river that required careful navigation.

One of the main challenges they faced was the dense vegetation, which made it difficult to see more than a few feet in any direction. This made it easy to lose sight of their surroundings, and they often had to rely on maps and compasses to stay on course.

Another challenge was the weather, which could change quickly and dramatically. The area was known for heavy rain and snowfall, which made it difficult to travel and set up camp. The research team had to be prepared for the harsh conditions. They carried heavy-duty rain gear and warm clothing to protect themselves from the elements, audio/video equipment, two laptops, cameras, and satellite equipment for data and communications.

The wilderness also had its fair share of wildlife, which could be dangerous. Tom, who would be carrying the shotgun, had to be on the lookout for bears, moose, and other large animals, which could be unpredictable and aggressive. They also had to be aware of smaller hazards like snakes, ticks, and poisonous plants, which could make their journey even more challenging.

Finally, the group had to be prepared for the isolation of the wilderness. They were far away from towns or cities, with no cell phone service or internet connection, other than a few spotty locations in the communities. They had to rely on Toms Ham Radio equipment, emergency locator beacons, and their skills and resources to survive and achieve their goal of finding the creature.

All in all, the Nass Valley wilderness was a formidable place, and they had to be at their best to navigate it and succeed in their search for the elusive creature.

Hairy man of the woods

Dr. Ross, Jenny and Tom arrived in *Gitlaxt'aamiks* to start their research expedition with a visit to the Nisga'a Museum. The visit to the museum was on the UBC's agenda as the first stop to learn more about this Hominid and view the exhibit Hli Goothl Wilp-Adokshl - Hairy man of the woods.

The Nisga'a Museum was a valuable resource for their research as it had a Sasquatch or Hairy man of the woods exhibit that was particularly interesting to Dr. Ross and Jenny. They were fascinated by the presentation as it displayed the cultural significance of Sasquatch to the Nisga'a people and the role it played in their beliefs and mythology.

Tom, a Sasquatch hunter, also visited the museums' Sasquatch exhibit. Tom was their connection to the Nass Valley, as he was well-versed in the area and had a vast knowledge of Sasquatch sightings. Tom shared his experiences and insights with Dr. Ross and Jenny, which added to their understanding of the elusive creature. They entered the museum and were greeted by the Curator. Dr. Lisa Ross introduced Jenny and Tom Miller to the curator.

The curator began the tour. "Welcome to our museum. The Nisga'a people are Indigenous people from the Nass River Valley in northern British Columbia, Canada.

The Nisga'a Nation comprises four villages: *Gitlaxt'aamiks* , Laxgalts'ap, Gitwinksihlkw, and Gingolx. Each village has its unique history, culture, and traditions, as well as its own elected government.

The Nisga'a people have a rich cultural heritage, including a complex social and political system, a distinctive language, and a deep connection to the land.

In 1998, the Nisga'a people signed the Nisga'a Treaty, which marked a significant step forward in the reconciliation process between Indigenous peoples and the Canadian government. This year in 2023 marks 25 years since its signing. Delegates are going to Ottawa in February for meetings. The treaty recognized Nisga'a self-government and established a framework for Nisga'a governance and administration and the protection of Nisga'a rights, culture, and traditions.

Today, the Nisga'a Nation is a thriving, self-governing community with a strong sense of pride and a commitment to preserving its cultural heritage. The Nisga'a people are involved in various economic and social activities, including forestry, fishing, tourism, and the arts. They continue to play a significant role in shaping the future of their communities and their nation.

The Nisga'a name for Sasquatch is Hli Goothl Wilp-Adokshl, which means "hairy man of the woods." The Nisga'a people have a long history of Sasquatch sightings and have passed down stories from generation to generation. The exhibit showcased the beliefs and stories associated with Sasquatch in the Nass Valley, which was a valuable resource for Dr. Ross and Jenny's research.

Dr. Ross and Jenny were impressed by the Nisga'a Museum's dedication to preserving the cultural heritage and history of the Nass Valley. The Sasquatch exhibit was a unique and eye-opening experience for them as they learned about the cultural significance of Sasquatch to the Nisga'a people. They were grateful for the opportunity to visit the museum and learn more about the subject of their research.

After the museum exhibition, they made a road trip to explore each village; Dr. Ross and Jenny learned about the unique history and customs of the indigenous communities in the area. At *Gitlaxt'aamiks*, the group spent the morning exploring the village and learning about its history from the residents. They visited the cultural center, which displayed artifacts and information about the Gitksan people and their customs.

In Laxgalts'ap, they were struck by the beauty of the coastline and learned about the Lax Kw'alaams people at the community center, which had a display of traditional clothing and artwork. At Gitwinksihlkw, the friendly residents welcomed the group. They performed and danced for the trio.

In Gingolx, the group spent the day exploring the village, witnessing a traditional dance performance, and trying local cuisine, Nisga'a soup. The soup is a cultural meal that they use for unique traditions. The road trip allowed Dr. Ross and Jenny to gain a deeper understanding of the cultural heritage and history of the Nass Valley and its people. They were grateful for the opportunity to learn about each village's unique traditions and the residents' dedication to preserving their heritage. This road trip was a valuable learning experience that left a lasting impression on the duo.

"I'm starting to tire out; we should get to the bed and breakfast, settle in for the evening, have dinner, then get a good sleep. We have a long tour in the morning. It's a five-hour excursion to the Lava Beds, Vetter Falls, and hot springs." Lisa said. "I concur. We had a busy day today; I have to get my reports carried out for today's events," Jenny said.

Guided Tour

The group met Roger, their guide, at 9 am. He was from the Nisga'a Nation and from Gitlaxt'aamiks, the largest Nisga'a village. He had the van ready for them. He drove Lisa, Jenny, Tom and another group of tourists to the Lava Beds, the tour's first destination. They drove to the beautiful old-growth forest of Anhluut'ukwsim Laxmihl Angwinga'asanskwhl Nisga'a Memorial Lava Bed Park.

Once they arrived at the first stop, Roger told them stories about the volcanic features and the Nisga'a culture as they walked. He said, "This park is unique because it shows both the natural and the cultural heritage of the Nisga'a people. It's the first park in BC that does that, and it's run by both the Nisga'a Nation and BC Parks."

Roger continued, "About 250 years ago, a cinder cone volcano called Tseax erupted on our lands. It belongs to a chain of more than 100 volcanoes that reaches Alaska. The lava flows from the eruption spread over 22.8 km and wiped out two villages and caused the death of around 2,000 Nisga'a people and their livestock.

The Nisga'a people have stories that tell about the eruption and how it affected them. The Tseax cone is not extinct and may erupt in the future. " "The Nisga'a alkali basalt flow, is one of the easiest-to-reach volcanic features in BC. Roger walked with the group through a beautiful old-growth forest and showed different volcanic features, such as the crater, the lava lake, and the lava tubes." Lisa asked, "Can you tell us more about the Nisga'a alkali basalt flow?"

"It's one of the youngest and most accessible volcanic features in

British Columbia. This guided tour offers visitors a chance to learn about the geological history of the area." Jenny asked, "What kind of interesting features can we expect to see on the hike?" "We'll be able to see a tree cast, which was formed by burned-out tree trunks leaving holes in the lava. We'll also see a lava tube, which was formed as the top layer cooled and hardened. And we'll see different types of lava flow such as pahoehoe, AA, and blocky."

Jenny asked, "How did the lava flow from the crater to the Tseax Valley?"

"The lava spilled from the crater an estimated 250 years ago and followed a creek bed down slope to Lava Lake and down the Tseax Valley to the Nass River. The lava travelled at different speeds depending on the steepness of the slope."

Dr. Ross said, "This is all so fascinating. Thank you for sharing this information with us." "It's my pleasure. I love sharing the history and culture of the Nisga'a people with visitors. I hope you all enjoy the hike!"

As they continued their hike, Dr. Ross, Jenny, and Tom were fascinated by the natural beauty and rich history of the Nisga'a Memorial Lava Bed Park, guided by the knowledgeable and passionate Nisga'a guide. They photographed the tree cast and the holes left after the lava burned out the tree trunks. It was a fantastic site to see. Tom photographed Lisa and Jenny by the tree cast. When they arrived at the Lava Tube, Jenny marvelled at the site. "Tom? Could you take our photo?" Tom agreed, then snapped ten photos in different locations.

Then the Nisga'a guide led the way to the hot springs, one of the attractions in the park. Dr. Lisa Ross, Jenny, and Tom Miller followed him through the forest, marvelling at the wild beauty of the place. They heard the birds singing, the leaves rustling, and the water flowing. "Follow me," the guide said, gesturing to a well-marked trail. "We're almost there." Jenny inhaled the crisp mountain air. "This is such a gorgeous place." Tom agreed. "And the hot springs are heavenly. I can't wait to soak in them and unwind." Lisa nodded. "I've read that the water is rich in minerals beneficial for your skin."

They reached the hot springs and saw the water bubbling and sparkling. The guide told them the story of the springs. "The Nisga'a people have used these hot springs for generations," the guide said. "They think that the water can heal and soothe various conditions." Jenny touched the water with her hand. "It's so warm." Tom agreed. "I'm with you on that. Let's go for a dip!" They immersed themselves in the hot springs, feeling the tension melt away. The other group members joined in and got in the water.

The guide watched them with a smile, happy to see them appreciate the natural wonder of the park. "This is a truly unique place," the guide said. "And I'm honoured to share it with visitors like you." When they were finished at the hot springs, the next journey was about to begin.

They arrived at the spectacular Vetter Falls, a waterfall shaped by the volcanic lava that cut through the Tseax Valley to the Nass River. "It's even more breathtaking than I recalled," Tom said, staring at the waterfall. "The Nisga'a people have a legend about the falls. They believe a mighty spirit resides in the falls and safeguards the land. The spirit is called Hli Goothl, the Guardian of the Waters." "That's captivating," Lisa said. "Can you tell us more about the legend?" "Sure," the guide said. "The legend says that Hli Goothl has the power to influence the water and is in charge of keeping the balance between the land and the water.

The Nisga'a people always have esteemed and honoured Hli Goothl and still do to this day." "That's incredible. Thank you for sharing the legend with us," Jenny said as the group continued to marvel at the waterfall. "You're welcome," the guide said. "I hope you all have had a wonderful time on this tour and learned something new about the Nisga'a culture and the remarkable volcanic landscape of this park."

Grizzly Survival

The next day After their visit to the Lava Beds national park, Lisa, Jenny, and Tom set out on their research project to study the Kermode Bear. They hiked the Lava Lake trail system and had been travelling for about an hour. They had a rest stop at this scenic spot, then continued hiking for one more hour before stopping at their first campsite for the night. There, they would set up their equipment to study the Kermode Bear and the unique ecosystems in the area. Tom broke out the food for their stop and got to cooking it right away. Then it was feasting time. After the half-hour break, they headed out on the trail for the first campsite.

The next part of the hike was a grueling climb to the midpoint of the mountain and then a descent to a hill overlooking a valley known to have Kermode bears. They set up camp and unpacked the audio/video equipment, tripods, parabolic directional microphone system and the data link to the satellite. After 20 minutes, the equipment was set up and ready for testing. Lisa booted up the laptops and waited for them to startup. After a few minutes, the laptops were up and working correctly, and she opened the apps needed for the data collection and transfer. She performed the test, and the signal was streaming live Data.

Lisa & Jenny started to collect the needed data about this location. Three Kermode bears were feasting on berries in a field, while two black bears were catching fish in the stream. They noticed three hunters out hunting for food around a half mile away. The hunters never even knew they were on Camera or audio for that fact. "This is the easy part; we just sit and enjoy the show," Lisa said. "Everything is done for us, Tom,"

Jenny replied. Tom asked, "it's that automated; nothing to do now?" "Yes, it is," Lisa said. "I'm going to get wood for the fire," Tom replied.

Tom gathered enough firewood and piled it next to the pit he dug out. He then retrieved rocks to go around the pit from the mountain they just came down from. He placed the stones around the pit and laid firewood into the hole. It was too early in the day for a fire, but it was ready for tonight's campfire.

Then from out of nowhere, the crack of the gun stung the air. Lisa pointed the camera at the hunters. "Looks like they shot a deer down there," Tom said as he looked at the video on the laptop. Lisa and Jenny saw the hunters closing in on the deer. The men searched the area where the deer went down. They found it 250 yards away. The hunters took the deer, tied the legs, hoisted it on a tree branch, and began dressing it.

Lisa re-pointed the camera back at the bears for her research. They collected four hours more data for UBC and then shut down the system and repacked the equipment for the hike in the morning. The sun was going down, and they moved their chairs closer to the fire pit for a night of relaxation by the fire. Tom got the fire started, and they sat around the warm fire and talked about the hike and events of the day. They listened to the wildlife filling the air, then climbed into their tents' warm sleeping bags.

The following day after breakfast, the trio broke camp and headed out to the next campsite. They took a different trail system that was an easy hike. "How many trails are around this area?" Jenny asked. "Miles and miles, most are connected to trap lines and go on forever. They even connect to other villages," Tom replied.

When they arrived at their second campsite, they were excited to set up camp and start the data collection again. The audio/video, laptops and satellite system was set up once more for the night, and they continued their research in the morning.

However, their peaceful evening was quickly interrupted when they heard strange noises from the surrounding woods.

At first, they thought it was just a wild animal in the distance, but as they listened more closely, they realized they heard a bear from a remote location away from the campsite.

But before they could even think about investigating more Kermode bears, they faced a much more immediate problem – a bear. A curious grizzly cub had wandered into their campsite and was quickly followed by its mother. The mother bear saw her cub too close to the group and charged at them, her mighty roar echoing through the forest. The cub returned to its mother, but she was still unsatisfied. She stood her ground and then charged again directly at the group. It was clear that she saw them as food.

Tom, who was carrying a shotgun, was ready for this situation. He aimed, his hands steady, and fired his first shot. The shot landed on the ground before the bear's feet, stopping it in its tracks. He fired another shot, and this scared the bear away. The group breathed a sigh of relief as they watched the mother grizzly disappear back into the forest with her cub.

The rest of the night was filled with excitement and fear as they heard the echo of a creature screaming in the distance, it filled the valley below, but they were safe and grateful for Tom's quick thinking in averting the bear attack.

They continued their journey the next day, heading to the base camp for the night before the hike to the hunters' cabin. Dr. Ross, Tom, and Jenny arrived at the spot for their base camp, excited for the adventure ahead. They began by unpacking their supplies and setting up their tents. Tom, who oversaw setting up the tents, called out to the group, "OK, everyone, let's get these tents set up before it gets dark." Jenny and Dr. Ross helped him stake the tents down and set up the rain fly.

As they were finishing up with the tents, Dr. Ross said, "Tom, can you and Jenny take care of hoisting the food cache into that tall tree over there? I want to ensure it's out of reach of bears or other animals."

Tom nodded and said, "Sure thing, Dr. Ross. We've got this." He and Jenny grabbed the rope and the food cache and set off toward the tree. Jenny asked, "How are we going to hoist it up?"

Tom replied, "We'll tie the rope around the cache, and then I'll climb the tree and tie the rope to a branch at the top. Then we'll pull it up."

They heard voices approaching as they hoisted the food cache into the tree. They turned to see four Nisga'a hunters approaching their camp. Dr. Ross greeted them and asked if they needed any help. The hunters smiled and said they were hunting moose and would like to stay the night just outside of the base camp.

Dr. Ross welcomed them, "Of course, you're welcome to stay the night here. We have enough room for everyone." The hunters thanked her and set up their camp outside the base camp.

That night, the Nisga'a hunters sat around the campfire and shared stories. Dr. Ross, Jenny, and Tom listened in awe to the hunters' tales of hunting in the wilderness and their knowledge of the area. "The elders passed down these stories through generations of our people about a creature known as the hairy man of the woods. They say it roams the forests and mountains and is as big as a bear but covered in hair. It is said to have a keen sense of smell and is extremely elusive."

Greg said, "I remember hearing from my grandfather about a hunting party that encountered the hairy man. They were tracking a deer when they stumbled upon a clearing where the creature was standing. It looked at them for a moment before disappearing into the forest."

Edward chimed in, "There are stories of hairy man stealing fish from our rivers and streams. The elders say that if you see him, you must leave immediately and not look back. He will follow you and bring bad luck to your village if you do."

Dan was next. "My great-grandmother told me of a time when a group of our people were lost in the mountains. They were on the brink of starvation when they came across a clearing filled with berries. They were able to survive because of those berries. When they returned to the village, they said they saw the hairy man watching over them."

It was a great way to learn about the culture and customs of the local people. As the night went on, they all retired to their tents, tired but excited for the days ahead.

The next day, the hunters took Dr. Ross, Jenny, and Tom out into the wilderness to show them the areas where they had encountered the hairy man. They pointed out the creature left tracks and other signs that they believed. "See here, and these are footprints that are too big to be from any animal we know of," one of the hunters said. "And you can see where it has been digging for roots or berries."

The group also came across a tree stripped of its bark, which the hunters attributed to the hairy man. "This is where he sharpens his claws," one of them said. "It's a sign that he's nearby."

Michael told the story about One hunter who told of a time when he and his hunting party had come across a pile of fish that had been left on a rock. "We knew it was from the hairy man. He had taken the fish from our rivers and left them as a gift," the hunter said.

The group also heard stories of the hairy man helping the Nisga'a people in times of need. Greg said One hunter told of a time when his village suffered from a severe drought. "We performed a ceremony to ask for the help of the hairy man, and the next day, it rained for the first time in months," he said.

Dr. Ross, Jenny, and Tom were in awe of the knowledge and experience that the hunters shared with them. As they sat around the campfire that night, they discussed what they had learned and reflected on the importance of respecting different cultures and belief systems.

Tom spoke up, "It's fascinating how different cultures have their own stories and beliefs about creatures that many of us might consider myths or legends. But for them, it's a part of their reality, and it's essential to understand and appreciate their perspective."

Jenny added, "I also think it's important to consider the impact that our actions have on the environment and the creatures that live in it. It's clear that the Nisga'a people have a deep connection to the land and the hairy man. It makes me think about how we can better protect and preserve our natural world."

Dr. Ross nodded in agreement, "Exactly. It's crucial to approach other cultures and beliefs with an open mind and a willingness to learn. We can all benefit from gaining a deeper understanding of different perspectives and ways of life."

As the night went on, the group continued their discussion, sharing their own stories and experiences. Michael recounted a time when he and his father had gone hunting, and they had stumbled upon a bear cub. "My dad said that we had to leave the cub alone, even though it was tempting to take it back with us. He explained that bears are a part of the ecosystem and play an important role in maintaining balance."

Lisa chimed in, "It's interesting how different cultures have their own beliefs and practices for living in harmony with nature. For example, the Nisga'a people believe in thanking the animals they hunt and using every part of the animal. It's a way of showing respect and appreciation for the life that was taken."

The group continued their conversation late into the night, and as they headed to bed, they felt a sense of camaraderie and connection that only comes from sharing a unique experience with others.

The next day, the group set out on a hike to explore more of the surrounding wilderness. They marveled at the rugged beauty of the landscape and the diverse array of plants and animals they encountered. They also kept an eye out for any signs of the hairy man, hoping to catch a glimpse of the creature they had heard so much about.

As they trekked deeper into the wilderness, they came across a clearing with a small stream running through it. There, they saw the hairy man for the first time. It was a surreal experience, and the group was at a loss for words. Lisa snapped dozens of photographs, and Jenny videoed it and what it was doing.

The creature seemed to be going about its business, foraging for food and tending to its surroundings. It didn't seem to notice the group, and after a few minutes, it disappeared into the trees. The group was left speechless, but they all knew that they had witnessed something incredible.

The encounter with the hairy man left the group in awe, and they spent the rest of their hike discussing what they had seen. They marvelled at the creature's size and strength and how it seemed to move easily through the wilderness.

Dr. Ross noted that their encounter reminded us how little we still know about the natural world. "For years, people have dismissed stories of creatures like the hairy man as mere folklore or imagination, but now we have proof that they exist. It makes you wonder what other mysteries are waiting to be discovered."

As they made their way back to camp, the group was met by several members of the Nisga'a community. They had heard about the group's encounter with the hairy man and had come to speak with them about their experience.

The Nisga'a people were overjoyed that the group had seen the creature and shared their stories and beliefs about the hairy man. They explained that the creature symbolized the connection between the people and the land and reminded them of the importance of living in harmony with nature.

The group immersed themselves in the Nisga'a culture, learning about their traditions, customs, and way of life. They visited a nearby village, took part in a traditional dance ceremony, feasted on local cuisine, and heard more stories about the hairy man.

Jenny was particularly drawn to the Nisga'a people's connection to the land and their efforts to preserve it. She asked one of the community leaders about their sustainability practices. They explained how they have always lived in harmony with the environment, using traditional methods to hunt, fish, and gather food. They emphasized the importance of giving back to the land and only taking what was needed to maintain balance.

Moved by what she had learned, Jenny suggested that the group organize a cleanup of the surrounding wilderness to give back to the land that had given them so much. The Nisga'a people were thrilled to hear of their idea and offered to help.

Together, the group and the community members spent the next few hours cleaning the area around their campsite, picking up litter that was left on the trail, and ensuring the natural surroundings were undisturbed. They also participated in reforestation, planting new trees in areas damaged by wildfires.

The group felt a deep sense of satisfaction and fulfillment as they worked. They had come to the wilderness to learn about the Nisga'a people and the hairy man. Still, they had also learned about preserving the environment and living in harmony with nature. They knew that their experience in the wilderness had changed them and that they would carry those lessons with them for the rest of their lives.

After the cleanup and reforestation efforts, the group and the Nisga'a community gathered for a final meal together. The atmosphere was joyful and celebratory as they feasted on fresh fish and locally grown produce and shared stories and laughter.

As the night wore on, the group began to reflect on their time in the wilderness. Dr. Ross commented, "It's amazing how a simple trip to explore the wilderness can be an incredible learning experience. We came here to learn about the hairy man and gained so much more. We learned about the importance of cultural preservation and environmental conservation."

Tom added, "And we also learned about the power of community and how coming together to work towards a common goal can be so rewarding. It's something we don't always get to experience in our day-to-day lives."

Jenny agreed, "I feel like we've not only gained a new perspective, but we've also made lasting connections with the Nisga'a people. It's a reminder of how much we have to gain when we take the time to learn about other cultures and traditions."

Tseax Volcano

Tom woke up at 5 am, eager to make a big breakfast for himself and his friends Lisa and Jenny. He knew that the smell of freshly brewed coffee and sizzling bacon would be enough to wake them up and entice them to come out of their tents. As he prepared a plate of hash browns, eggs, bacon, and toast, he couldn't help but think about how delicious the meal would be. The smell of breakfast was filling the air, making its way through the crisp morning air, and Tom knew that Lisa and Jenny would soon be joining him.

As he sat at the campfire, sipping on his first cup of coffee, he could hear the sound of rustling tents. "The coffee smells great," said Lisa as she emerged from her tent, rubbing the sleep from her eyes. Tom smiled, knowing he had succeeded in waking her up with the aroma of his delicious breakfast.

Jenny, however, was still sound asleep, completely unaware of the delicious meal waiting for her. "Hey, Jenny? Time to wake up. Tom made us breakfast, hurry or you get none," said Lisa, trying to shake her awake.

"One more hour, please?" replied Jenny, still half asleep. "We have other things to do other than sleep," said Tom, trying to get her up and moving.

Jenny slowly kicked off her sleeping bag and started to get up. "All right, I'm coming, getting up," she said, groggily making her way to her hiking shoes. She knew that if she didn't hurry, she would miss out on the delicious breakfast that Tom had prepared for them.

The meal was delicious and filling, the perfect start to a long day of hiking. Tom and Lisa discussed their upcoming trip to the hunter's cabin as they cleaned up and packed up their backpacks along with their video and audio gear. Tom was anxious about the trip, as there had been credible witness accounts of a mysterious creature around the area. Four people had reported seeing a large, hairy creature on the trails, but no one had been able to provide any proof.

On the other hand, Lisa was excited about getting extensive audio/video evidence of the creature. She was determined to get to the bottom of the mystery, prove to the university and write a piece that would be printed in the science journal that the new hominid species creature was real. Tom, however, needed to be more sure they would be safe, which was his responsibility. He was worried they would be putting themselves in danger if they were not careful, but Lisa was adamant that they try to get more evidence that the creature existed.

With full stomachs and happy hearts, they set off on their hike. The smell of breakfast and coffee still lingered in the air. As Dr. Ross, Jenny, and Tom hiked, Tom can't help but marvel at the stunning view from where they are standing. He expresses his excitement to see the Tseax and the cabin in their research trip. Jenny agrees, pointing out that the area's beauty makes it hard to imagine the destruction caused by the Tseax volcano's eruption around 250 years ago.

Dr. Ross reminds them of the significance of the eruption and its impact on the Nisga'a communities, which resulted in the destruction of two villages and the death of 2,000 people from poison gas. Tom reflects on the tragedy of the event, finding it hard to comprehend the scale of destruction and loss of life, but they did see the lava fields, which was a vast sight to behold. He expresses gratitude for the opportunity to hike safely in the area today. "Let's be careful and watch ourselves. This forest can be dangerous, OK?"

Jenny agreed, pointing out that the experience serves as a reminder of nature's power and unpredictability. As they continue to hike, Dr. Ross highlights the geologic evidence of the eruption, such as the cinder cones and other volcanic features, that they will be able to see firsthand.

Tom observes that the cinder cones are unique and different from other volcanic rock formations he has seen. Jenny agrees, and they both find it fascinating to think about how the volcano created them through repeated eruptions. Dr. Ross reminds them that the Tseax volcano is still active and could potentially erupt again in the future.

This thought is sobering, but Tom finds it makes the hike all the more exciting as it is a chance to witness the ongoing geological processes shaping our planet. The group continues to hike with a newfound appreciation for the natural world.

Suddenly, a roar echoes through the forest. The group of hikers, who were previously enjoying their trek through the wilderness, froze in fear. The sound started getting closer and closer. A series of loud whacks is heard from a nearby tree as they begin to panic. The hikers quickly look around, trying to identify the noise source.

Terrified, they realize that the noise is coming from their left. Without hesitation, they begin to search for a place to hide. They scan the area, looking for a cave, a large rock, or even a dense thicket to conceal themselves. They move as quickly and quietly as possible, not wanting to attract the predator's attention.

As they run, their hearts pounding, they come across a large boulder. Without hesitation, they huddle behind it, trying to make themselves as small as possible. They hold their breath, waiting. The minutes tick by, and the noise gradually fades into the distance, signaling that the danger has passed.

"What the hell was that? Did you hear it? It sounded like something big." Jenny exclaims as she looks around nervously. Jenny trembles and asks, "What do you think it was?" Tom is shaken and replies, "I think it's probably what we're looking for. It sounded like a Sasquatch roar to me." "Really?" Jenny's voice is filled with disbelief. "They do that?" she says as she tries to process the information. "I had no idea." Lisa, also shaking and trembling, her words broken as she was scared, replied. "The Nisga'a people call it the Nax Nok. A supernatural spirit. It's a cryptid." Jenny asks her voice trembling with fear. "Do you think that's what we just heard?" Dr. Ross: "It's possible, but we can't be sure until we investigate further. Let's go toward the sound and see what we can find."

    The three start carefully, cautiously, and slowly without a sound, start walking towards the sound of the animal's roar. Then they hear another series of thwacks of a tree. "Friken hell," Tom blurts out. This stops them in their tracks. Lisa states, "I think we should just stay here and try to get audio and video?" Then a whooping sound fills the air. "Agreed, we stay here for a bit. Hopefully, we catch it on video." Tom slings his shotgun from his side into a ready position. They crouch down, trying not to be seen. Again, a loud series of thwacks, and whooping from the Sasquatch.

    Tom hears and see's the trees shaking as something big runs away from the area. The creature's heavy footsteps can be heard as it moves quickly through the forest, making it clear that it is in a hurry to escape. "Look, over there," he points." "I see the trees moving. That is a mighty big being," Lisa exclaims." "Me too. Wow, this thing moves fast, and it's distancing itself away from us," Jenny says, still crouched down. Tom cannot help but feel a sense of awe and wonder that the legendary creature is close to them and moving away so fast.

    Despite his uncertainty, Tom feels a sense of excitement as he watches the trees shake as Sasquatch disappears into the forest. As the Sasquatch disappears from their view, the three take a moment to catch their breath and process what just happened. Tom's heart is racing, and his hands are shaking from the adrenaline rush. "That was incredible," he says, still in awe of what they just witnessed. Jenny nods in agreement, her eyes wide with excitement and fear. "I can't believe it. I wish we got to lay eyes on it," she says. "I never thought we'd get so close to one this soon."

Dr. Ross, who has remained relatively calm throughout the encounter, suggests they follow and see if they can find further evidence of its presence. The three set out, tracking the creature's last direction of travel, and studying the signs of its passing. They find broken branches, crushed foliage, trees thrown to the ground and even tufts of hair caught on a downed tree branch. Lisa stopped and crouched down as she reached into her sample bag, took out a sample container, took her tweezers, and collected the hair, examining it closely. She puts it into her collection container and then into the bag. "It stinks, and it is very oily," She stated. "The oil must be a protective layer from the snow and rain. Like a dog's oily fur." Jenny replied, "yes, it sure does stink."

They came across a clearing with large, unusual footprints as they followed the tracks. The three researchers exchange excited glances as they realize that these are the footprints of Sasquatch. They quickly take measurements, photographs, and castings of the footprints before continuing on their journey. As the day wears on, the three continue to track the Sasquatch, following its trail deeper into the forest. Lisa knows their discovery could change how people think about Sasquatch and the possibility of a hominid discovery.

They know they have much work to do, analyzing the collected data and planning their next steps. But for now, they have some evidence. They have more than just an opportunity to witness a legendary creature, Sasquatch.

The sun was starting to set, and Tom suggested they camp here for the night. They had been hiking for a few hours and were all feeling the effects of the long day. The area was beautiful, next to a stream, and there was plenty of space to set up camp. Lisa agreed with Tom, and the three began setting up for the night, clearing an area for the tents, gathering firewood, and ensuring the supplies were secure. Once everything was set, Tom started a fire, then went fishing. After an hour of fishing he emerged from the trees with a string of fish. He had caught enough fish for their dinner, cooked it, then they all ate by the fire, discussing their hike.

In the morning, they woke up early and had a quick breakfast before resuming their hike. They were refreshed from a good night's sleep and were excited to continue their journey. The crew packed up the camp and started on the trail again, taking in the beauty of the morning light. They knew it would be a long day, but they were ready and energized to take on the next leg of this journey.

Tom was the first to speak, "That's the closest I have ever been to a Sasquatch." Lisa nodded in agreement. "I know, it's still hard for me to believe. But the evidence we collected, the video and pictures, the footprints and castings, the hair samples, it's all there. We have some proof that Sasquatch exists. But still, it is not enough for science." She took a sip from her water bottle, her hands visibly slightly shaking.

Jenny, who had been quiet most of the morning, spoke up, "I know it's exciting, but it's also a little scary. I mean, we were almost face-to-face with a Sasquatch."

Dr. Ross, who had been listening to jenny, chimed in, "It means that there's still so much we don't know about our planet. And that there's still so much to discover and explore. This opportunity allows us to study a creature many think was just a legend. It may turn out that it is truly a new being. This discovery of a new hominid will be astounding to the community." Tom nodded, "Yeah, and I can't wait to see what else we find out about this thing. I mean, I always knew Sasquatch was real, but what else is out there that we don't know about?"

Lisa agreed, "I know, it's exciting to think about. But we must be careful and respectful of the creature and its habitat. We don't want to harm it or disturb its environment."

Jenny nodded, "I agree. And we also have to consider the impact this discovery will have on the world. People will have many questions, and we must be prepared to answer them."

Dr. Ross nodded, "Exactly. And that's why we must conduct our research responsibly and ethically. We have a responsibility to not only study Sasquatch but also to educate the public about it."

Tom checked his GPS to see the exact location they were at. They had been hiking for an hour, so they took a break. They came across a group of hikers, and a Nisga'a guide hiking on their way back to the lava bed to the parked bus. The hikers, who looked tired and a little disheveled, stopped to inform them that they had heard strange noises, tree whacks, and whooping sounds while coming down the trail. They also saw bears eating in a berry field about two kilometers up the trail.

The guide advised them to be cautious and make noise as they walked to avoid surprising the bears, and to be watchful of the spirits in the trees.

After their break, they continued with the hike, taking the warning into account. They saw two deer and took photos while hiking. About an hour they reached the berry field where the bears were reported to be. They saw no bears, but they could see the signs of where the bears were eating in the bushes. The group felt grateful for the warning and more prepared for any encounter they might have with the bears; besides, Tom was armed. They continued their hike, ensuring to keep on the trail.

As they hiked further, the trail became steeper and more challenging. The group had to navigate through rocky terrain and dense foliage, making it harder for them to keep their pace. After a few hours, they finally reached the summit, and the view took their breath away. The vast expanse of wilderness was spread out before them, and they could see for miles in all directions.

They decided to take a break and rest before starting their descent.

They sat down to catch their breath and take in the view. Tom pulled out his binoculars and scanned the area, hoping to spot any wildlife. After a few minutes, he saw something moving in the distance.

"Hey guys, look over there," Tom said, pointing towards a clearing in the distance.

The group looked through the binoculars and saw a group of caribou grazing in the clearing. They watched in silence, not wanting to disturb the peaceful scene. After a few minutes, the caribou moved on, disappearing into the wilderness.

Jenny let out a deep sigh, "I wish we could stay up here forever."

Dr. Ross smiled, "As much as I would love to, we still have to make it back down to camp before sunset."

As they started their descent, they realized that the way down was even more challenging than the climb up. They had to take it slowly and carefully, making sure not to slip on the rocks or lose their footing on the steep terrain. They used their walking sticks for support, as Tom was leading the way down.

After a while, they came across a stream, and they took another break to refill their water bottles. While they were resting, they heard a strange noise coming from the forest. It sounded like someone or something was knocking on a tree.

"What was that?" Jenny asked, looking around nervously.

"It could be Sasquatch," Dr. Ross suggested.

"But the hikers we met earlier mentioned hearing tree knocks," Tom added, his hand on his shotgun.

The group grew silent, trying to listen for any more sounds. They heard the noise again, but it was louder and more distinct this time.

"That's not a woodpecker," Jenny said, trembling. "We should keep moving."

The group quickly gathered their belongings and continued down the trail. The knocking stopped after a few minutes, and they didn't hear anything else for the rest of the descent.

As they arrived back at camp, they were greeted by the warm glow of a campfire and the smell of fresh food. There were a small group of Nisga'a there and they were camping. Hi, I am Emma. Lisa introduced themselves to Emma and her friends. Emma and the other Nisga'a had prepared food over the campfire, they asked Lisa, Jenny, and Tom to join them, and they all sat down together to share stories and experiences from their day.

"We saw a group of caribou on the summit," Jenny said excitedly.

Emma smiled, "They are beautiful creatures, aren't they? The caribou is a sacred animal for our people. It represents endurance and resilience."

Dr. Ross nodded, "They are fascinating. There are so many different species of animals living in the forest."

The group discussed their encounter with the strange knocking sound on the descent as they ate. Emma listened intently and nodded knowingly.

"That sound you heard could have been the hairy man," Emma said.

"The hairy man," Jenny said, "we saw the hairy man display at the museum."

"Yes, the hairy man is a legend of our people. It is said to be a creature that lives in forests and mountains. Some say it's a Sasquatch, hairy man, while others believe it's a supernatural being. We call it a Nax Nok"

The group sat in awe, listening to Emma and what she was saying.

"People have reported hearing knocking sounds, whooping, tree branches snapping, and whistling in the woods, which they attribute to the hairy man. But don't be afraid. You have nothing to fear as long as you respect the land and the spirits that inhabit it."

The group continued to listen to the stories Emma told, mesmerized by the rich cultural history of the Nisga'a people. Dr. Ross was especially interested in the Nisga'a beliefs and traditions and asked many questions about their customs and practices.

Emma was happy to share her knowledge and spoke about the importance of maintaining a connection with nature and respecting the spirits that inhabit it. She talked about how her people had lived in harmony with the land for generations and believed that everything in nature was interconnected.

As they talked, the fire crackled, and the stars twinkled in the sky above. The group felt a sense of peace and contentment, surrounded by the beauty of the wilderness and the warmth of the campfire.

After the meal, the group retired to their tents, tired but exhilarated from the day's adventures. They fell asleep quickly, listening to the sounds of the forest and the gentle rustling of the leaves.

The next day, the group woke up early and explored more of the area. They hiked through dense forests, crossed rivers, and climbed steep hills, all while marveling at the landscape's beauty.

As they were hiking, they encountered a group of Nisga'a people fishing on the nearby river. The group stopped to watch as the Nisga'a expertly caught fish using traditional techniques.

Emma explained that fishing is an essential part of the Nisga'a culture and that they believed in taking only what they needed from the land. She spoke about the importance of preserving natural resources and ensuring that they were not overused or depleted.

The group continued their hike, taking in the sights and sounds of the wilderness. They saw eagles soaring overhead, beavers building dams in the rivers, and bears foraging for food in the forests. They felt a deep sense of awe and reverence for the natural world around them and were grateful for the opportunity to experience it in such a profound way.

As the day drew close, the group returned to camp, tired but happy. They sat around the campfire again, sharing stories and reflecting on their experiences.

"I never realized how much I took nature for granted," Jenny said, looking around at the trees and the stars.

"I know what you mean," Tom said. "I feel like I've gained a whole new appreciation for the beauty of the wilderness."

Dr. Ross nodded, "It's easy to forget how interconnected we are with nature. We must remember to treat the land and the creatures inhabiting it with respect and care."

Emma smiled, "That's the essence of our culture. We believe that everything in nature is connected and that we are responsible for protecting it for future generations."

The group shared more stories as the night wore on, sang songs, performed a ceremonial dance, and laughed together. They felt a sense of connection that they had never experienced before.

The next day, the group said their goodbyes to Emma and the Nisga'a people and started back on their journey.

"I'll never forget this experience," Jenny said, tears welling up in her eyes.

"Me neither," Lisa said, hugging her friend.

Jenny nodded, "It's an incredible journey. I feel like I've grown and learned so much about myself and the world around me."

Dr. Ross smiled, "That's the power of nature. It has a way of teaching us lessons that we could never learn in a classroom or a book. We need to remember to honour and respect it in our daily lives." The group walked on. Each lost in their thoughts and reflections on the journey they had.

Emergency Extraction

Jenny asked Lisa and Tom as they were walking through the forest. "Do you hear that?" "Yes, I hear it too," Lisa says, looking around for the source of the yelling. Tom nods in agreement, "It sounds like it's coming from over there," he points towards a dense area of trees. They start walking toward the voice. The three of them quicken their pace, following the faint sound of the wailing cries. As they get closer, a man's voice becomes louder and more distinct. Jenny's heart races as she realizes that someone is in danger.

They arrive at a densely forested area, and discover a man writhing in pain on the forest floor. "What the hell happened to you?" "I was fishing by the river when I heard a deep growling in the trees. I looked around but found nothing. Then the trees began to shake, and I noticed a large dark shape emerge from the bushes. I froze as its eyes fixed on me, then charged forward, then it came to a halt just a few feet away and stared at me, growling louder. I backed away slowly from the river and toward the trail. It then began throwing rocks, first small rocks, then bigger rocks. When one flew over my head, I ducked to protect myself. But another rock was heading straight for me, and it was too late. That rock on the ground, over there, smacked into my leg. "I believe it's broken." As he lay on the ground, unable to move or get up, he screamed in agony.

Dr. Lisa quickly reached into her backpack for the first aid kit and began assessing the man's injuries. She discovered he had a broken leg in three places and immediately began splinting it with the first aid kit and other supplies in the bag.

Tom began looking for materials to make a makeshift stretcher as they worked to stabilize the man's leg. He discovered two tree trunks on the ground, took out his saw from his backpack, cut it to the appropriate length, and began constructing a stretcher to transport the injured man out of the woods. Jenny assisted Tom by retrieving the rope from her backpack, cutting it to length, and then tying the rope to the trunks of the trees Tom had cut to secure the man in place.

After assembling the stretcher and securing the man, Tom took his radio from his backpack and dialed 911.

He used a phone patch to communicate with the logging repeater, relaying their location as well as the man's injuries.

An ambulance was quickly dispatched to the Lava Beds parking area to meet them.

Lisa, Jenny, and Tom carefully lifted the man onto the stretcher and began carrying him out of the woods as the ambulance was en route to the Nass Valley.

The terrain was rough and uneven, and the man was in a lot of pain, but they were determined to get him out of there safely.

They finally arrived at the parking lot, where the ambulance was waiting.

Paramedics arrived quickly, and loaded the man onto a gurney, transporting him to the Nisga'a Valley Health Authority building in Gitlaxt'aamiks, New Aiyansh, then drove off, as the siren wailed.

Dr. Ross, Jenny, and Tom jumped into Tom's truck and followed the ambulance.

As the ambulance pulled up to the NVHA in New Aiyansh, the paramedics quickly unloaded the injured man and rushed him into the emergency room. The staff at NVHA were well-prepared and immediately began to assess the man's injuries, taking note of his broken leg and any other injuries he may have sustained.

Dr. Ross, Jenny, and Tom, arrived a few minutes later and made their way to the emergency room quickly.

They gave the nurse on shift a detailed report on the man's condition, including information about how a Sasquatch threw a large rock at the man, which is how he sustained his injuries, and the treatment that had been provided in the field.

"A what threw a rock at him?" said the Doctor.

"Sasquatch."

Tom responded.

The Doctor had a perplexed look on his face. "I will write that on his chart," the doctor said, then scribbled it down on the patient's chart.

Soon after the injured man was brought in, a police officer arrived at the hospital. He questioned Dr. Ross, Jenny, and Tom, about what had occurred and how the man had been injured. Tom, who had called 911, filled the officer in on the details of the incident, including where they discovered the man, and the injuries he had sustained.

The emergency room staff quickly began treating the man's broken leg, properly setting it, and giving him an injection of pain medication to help manage the pain. They also conducted a thorough examination to rule out any other injuries and ensure the man's stability.

As the man's condition stabilized, the NVHA staff began preparing him for surgery. They requested an orthopedic surgeon and a team of nurses and anesthesiologists from Mills Memorial Hospital in Terrace to repair the man's broken leg. The situation was relayed to BCEMS by Mills Memorial's on-duty nurse. BCEMS said they would leave the hospital helipad in 45 minutes.

Three hours later, the orthopedic surgical team arrived by helicopter, and was driven to the NVHA building. While viewing the chart, the surgeon was briefed on the patient's progress, and the team scrubbed up and got to work. "A Sasquatch? You don't say?"

The operation went well, and the man's broken leg was properly set and secured. Throughout the procedure, the man's vital signs were closely monitored, and the medical team was able to keep him stable and comfortable.

Following surgery, the man was transferred to a private room for recovery and further monitoring. The nurses closely monitored his vital signs and gave him the care and medication he needed to recover.

Dr. Ross and the other medical personnel visited the man on a regular basis to ensure his comfort and to keep him informed of his condition. They also kept in touch with his family and kept them updated on his progress. He turned out to be the brother of the Chief of Gingolx.

As the man's condition improved, the NVHA staff began to make plans for his discharge. They provided him with information and instructions on how to care for his leg, and provided a list of follow-up appointments with the orthopedic surgeon in Terrace.

Finally, the man was released from the hospital and returned home to recover. He was grateful for the prompt and professional care he had received from the NVHA staff and was eager to return to his village.

The officer who was questioning Dr. Ross, Jenny, and Tom about the incident in the woods decided to tell them about an experience he had a few years ago while driving on the Nisga'a highway. He explained that he was on patrol and driving down the highway when he noticed something out of the ordinary.

He claimed to have seen a "Sasquatch" like creature jump over the highway about 500 meters in front of his car. He pulled over and got out to look for the creature, but it had vanished into the trees. He lingered for about fifteen minutes, hoping to catch a glimpse of what he'd just witnessed, but it was nowhere to be found.

He claimed that at first, he thought he had seen a large animal, but as he looked closer, he realized it couldn't be a bear or any other animal he was familiar with. The creature was covered in hair and looked unlike anything he had ever seen before.

He couldn't believe what he saw, and was rendered speechless as he attempted to make sense of the strange encounter. He described the creature as standing about 10 feet tall, and having large hairy arms. It had long hairy powerful legs, and jumped over the highway like nothing.

After the encounter, the police officer did some research, and discovered it was a Sasquatch, a legendary supernatural creature in the Nisga'a Nation. He discovered that it is a creature with the ability to jump great distances and move at incredible speeds. He was surprised to learn that the creature he had seen was a part of local stories.

He claimed he never forgot the strange encounter, and has often reflected on it over the years. He had never seen anything like it before, and was convinced that it was not a figment of his imagination.

He said he never saw the creature again, but he kept his eyes peeled for it on his patrols. He also spoke with other officers, but no one had ever witnessed anything like it. He also mentioned that a few of the elders had seen the creature in the area, so he assumed it was a rare sight.

The officer went on to say that he had always been skeptical of Sasquatch's existence, but after his encounter, he couldn't deny that something unusual had occurred. He'd never seen anything like it before, and he had no idea why.

He claimed that he had never reported the encounter because he was afraid of being mocked or dismissed. He was afraid the police would think he was crazy, but he felt compelled to tell his story to Dr. Ross, Jenny, and Tom, who had recently gone through a similar experience.

Dr. Ross, Jenny, and Tom were captivated by the officer's description of the strange creature. They were surprised to learn that the officer had seen it in person. The officer went on to say that he had always been fascinated by Sasquatch and other Nisga'a Nation legends. He had watched Sasquatch videos on YouTube and read numerous books and articles about it after his encounter.

He stated that he believed Sasquatch was a real creature, and that it was one of many creatures that exist in the world that science has yet to discover. He believed that there were many other undiscovered creatures out there. Dr. Ross, who had been paying close attention to the police officer's story, decided to tell him why they were in the woods that day. She explained that they were searching the area by hiking to the Tseax cone volcano and a hunter's cabin. She explained that they were on a mission to find Sasquatch and prove its existence to science.

The officer was taken aback when he learned that they were looking for Sasquatch, but Dr. Ross went on to explain that there had been numerous sightings of the creature in the area and that they had been studying the reports for years. She stated that they had heard stories of a creature 8 to 10 feet tall, and his story matched the Sasquatch description.

Dr. Ross went on to say they heard a man's cries today. They ran after the sound and discovered the man on the ground with a broken leg. They gave him first aid and assisted him in getting out of there safely.

The police officer was impressed with Dr. Ross's knowledge of the Sasquatch and was interested in sharing more about the creature. Dr. Ross was happy to share her research with the officer. Dr. Ross showed him pictures and videos of the Sasquatch they had taken the previous day.

Dr. Ross explained that the UBC team had been researching Sasquatch for years but had never found any evidence of the creature's existence until now. She stated that they discovered large footprints and took foot castings as well as hair samples that matched the description of the creature. Then they photographed and videotaped Sasquatch near a riverbank the day before, then it vanished into the woods.

The officer stated that he had been collaborating with local Nisga'a Nations communities to learn more about Sasquatch. The officer stated that the Nisga'a people had a wealth of knowledge, and stories about the creature, and had been extremely helpful and supportive.

He also stated that they were extremely respectful of the creature, and the land, and that they had no intention of harming the creature in any way. They were simply attempting to learn more about it, and comprehend its existence in the world.

The officer was impressed by Dr. Ross's dedication, and enthusiasm for Sasquatch, and thanked her for sharing their photographs, and video research with him.

"Hello, my name is Skyler Kane. "I'm a police officer assigned to the Aiyansh police department," he introduced himself, extending his hand to shake theirs.

The three of them shook his hand one after the other. Officer Kane explained. "I have extensive wilderness survival experience, and can provide protection, and support for your group. If you could use me in your research, that is."

Dr. Ross, Jenny, and Tom exchanged glances as they considered his offer. "We'd be delighted to have you join us," Dr. Ross said. "Your knowledge and experience will be invaluable to the group."

Tom and Jenny agreed, and the four of them left the hospital for Officer Kane's house. He retrieved his backpack, a rifle, some dehydrated packaged food, and some military MRE's.

"I always like to be prepared for any situation," Officer Kane said as he piled his belongings into the group's vehicle. "It's critical to have the right equipment and supplies in the wilderness."

The group began their journey. They arrived at their base camp, and he demonstrated how to set up a secure perimeter. Officer Kane pulled out his maps and satellite imagery of the surrounding area as they settled into their camp.

He explained that they needed to be on the lookout for any signs of unusual activity. He also warned them about wild animals, poisonous plants, and treacherous terrain in the area. Officer Kane began to share some of his stories, and experiences with the group, as they settled in for the night. He described some of the encounters he'd heard from others with Sasquatch in the past, as well as how he'd been taught to track and understand the creature's movements. He described how the Nisga'a Nations people assisted him in understanding Sasquatch culture, and how they valued it as a component of the ecosystem.

Officer Kane's knowledge and experience captivated the group, and they listened intently. They talked about their plans for the next day and how they planned to continue their search for Sasquatch. They planned to hike to Hunter's Cabin from base camp in the morning. They all eventually fell asleep as the night progressed, each with their own thoughts about the creature, and what they might encounter the next day.

The four set out the next morning to hike to the hunter's cabin. It was a two-hour hike, and with all the gear they were carrying, it would take some time to get there.

Officer Kane took the lead, with Tom close behind. They kept an eye out for Sasquatch activity, scanning the surrounding terrain for tracks or disturbances. Jenny and Lisa trailed behind, their gaze fixed on the bushes, trees, and the trail behind them, ready for any signs of the creature.

They came across several streams, and creeks while hiking, and Officer Kane demonstrated how to filter water and safely drink from it. He also pointed out various plant species, explaining which were edible and which were poisonous. Officer Kane, and the trio took regular breaks to rest and hydrate themselves.

As they continued their journey, they came across a clearing in the forest formed by trees that had been pushed down and snapped in half. Officer Kane recognized the signs right away and summoned the group to investigate.

"This is a common location for Sasquatch activity," he explained. "These trees have been pushed over with incredible force, and the creature has most likely been feeding here."

The group looked around, examining the broken trees and imagining the strength required to snap them in half.

They hiked through dense forests, treacherous mountains, and icy rivers, always on the lookout for the elusive creature. They didn't come across any other dangerous animals, but they did come across a few other hikers on the trails. They paused for a brief moment to converse with the hikers.

Sam, one of the hikers, claimed to have had a close encounter with the creature a few years ago. He described how he was camping alone in the woods when he heard strange noises outside his tent. He opened the flap to find a massive, hairy creature standing just a few feet away. He claimed that the creature let out a guttural roar before walking away into the forest. He ran out of the forest leaving his tent and belongings right where the were. The group listened intently to Sam's story, nodding in agreement with his description of the creature's size and behavior.

The Hunter's Cabin

Lisa, Jenny, Tom, and officer Kane had finally reached the hunter's cabin after a grueling hike. As they stepped inside, a sense of relief washed over them.

Lisa: "Wow, this place is perfect! We have everything we need here." Jenny: "Yes, let's get to work." The audio and video equipment, tripods, a parabolic directional microphone system, and the data link to the satellite were all taken out of their packs once again. It took about 30 minutes to set up everything for testing, being they were a bit bushed from the hiking. Lisa turned on the laptops and waited for them to start up. "My legs are so sore. I have never hiked that much in my life," Jenny said. Lisa replied, "I know. Mine are done as well. However, we can rest for the next few days after this is completed." After a short while, the laptops were functioning correctly, and she launched the necessary applications to collect and transfer data. Lisa proceeded with the test, and the signal successfully streamed live data.

Jenny and Lisa started setting up trail cameras and microphones along the surrounding trails. Tom and Officer Kane got the generator set up. The girls spent three hours carefully positioning the equipment to capture any sign of the Sasquatch.

Lisa: "This is it! This is where we'll catch some evidence. I can feel it." Jenny: "Me too. I am so happy this part is finally done. Let's get back to the cabin and check the feeds on the laptops."

As they returned to the cabin, they were exhausted but proud of their hard work. Both girls reached the cabin door, opened it, and hit the couch, just drained. Tom and Skyler were sitting at the table, drinking their coffee. They also were beaten by the hike. But the girls did it harder with the three-hour outdoor setup.

Knock knock

Tom walked to the door, and opened it. He saw a man in a forestry uniform standing on the porch. "Can I help you?" Tom asked.

"Hi, I'm James, a forestry worker from the Nisga'a Valley Forest Service. Is it okay if I come in?" James said.

"Sure, come on in," Tom replied, stepping aside to let James enter. "What brings you here today?" Tom asked, closing the door behind them. "I am doing my rounds, and I saw in the logbook that the UBC Department of Anthropology set up a reservation at the cabin for the week. "Yes, I am Dr. Lisa Ross from UBC. We are conducting research here for the week." Lisa chimed in. "Ah, great, very lovely to meet you. Our Nation is pleased to have you and your team visit our incredible spiritual lands." "The Nisga'a Nation is beautiful. We have been hiking and gathering research on the Kermode Bear, but we are looking for more conclusive evidence of Sasquatch so we can prove to our department that they do indeed exist."

Tom: "Would you like a cup of coffee?" James: "Sure, thank you."

James and Lisa were deep in conversation when they heard a knock at the door. "Busy place, I wonder who that could be," Lisa said

"I'll go check it out," James said, getting up from his seat.

As James approached the door, Lisa couldn't help but feel curious. She followed him to the entrance just in time to see James open the door to reveal three men from Gitwinksihlkw.

"Hey, how can I help you?" James asked.

"Good evening. We're on a hunting trip and wondered if it would be possible for us to stay the night at the cabin," one of the men said.

Lisa listened to their conversation and realized they had nowhere to stay for the night. "James, there's plenty of space here, and they seem like they could use a good place to rest after their hike," Lisa said.

James thought about it for a moment and agreed. "Sure, come on in. There's plenty of room," he said, stepping aside to let the men in.

There was enough room for everyone, so Lisa, Jenny, Tom, and Kane shook the men's hands and welcomed the three men and showed them around the cabin. The men found a room each and settled into their rooms for a much-needed rest after their journey.

Kane: "I'm going to chop some more wood for tonight." Then Officer Kane opened the door and went outside to chop wood for the fireplace.

Lisa: "We need to stay focused. Our goal is to find more proof of Sasquatch." Tom: "Agreed. We're in the right place for it. Let's make the most of it." Just then, Officer Kane came in with a pile of firewood, placed it near the fireplace, and went back out for another load.

Tom started to make a fire in the fireplace. After ten minutes, the warmth was starting to feel good on the girls. The crackling fire provided a comforting ambiance, adding to their resolve to unravel the mystery of Sasquatch. Jenny: "The fire is so cozy. It makes me even more determined to solve this mystery." As the night set in, Tom, Lisa, and Jenny huddled around the fireplace to discuss their plans for the next few days.

As the night grew darker, James and the three men from Gitwinksihlkw joined Lisa, Jenny, Tom, and officer Kane by the fireplace. "Hi, I am Dr. Lisa Ross from UBC. This is Jenny, also from UBC. We are here researching Sasquatch." Lisa told the men. "Hello, Dr. Ross and Jenny. It is nice to meet you. I am Don, this is my brother John, and this is Gerald, my cousin. We threw the net into the river and caught a few salmon. I hope everyone is hungry." They already knew Officer Kane and Tom. The two men from Gitwinksihlkw took each chair and placed them by the fireplace. John was cleaning the fish for dinner. Then the two men started to tell stories about what the elders in their community had passed down about Sasquatch. They spoke of sightings and encounters with the mysterious creature, piquing everyone's interest.

John was cooking a delicious salmon feast for the group. The aroma of the salmon filled the cabin, making everyone's mouth water. As they ate, they all shared stories and laughter, bonding over their common goal of finding evidence of Sasquatch.

After dinner, the group shared some of their personal Sasquatch experiences. Tom shared his first childhood encounter, and how it sparked his interest in the creature. Lisa spoke about her and Jenny taking photos, and videos of Sasquatch by the river the other day, then she told them of her research and how she became involved in the search for Sasquatch. James and the men from Gitwinksihlkw shared some of their encounters, which only added to the excitement and anticipation of their investigation.

A loud knock on the door interrupted the peaceful atmosphere as the group sat around the fire, chatting, and exchanging stories. James, closest to the door, got up to see who it was. He cautiously opened the door, but there was no one there. Kane asked, "who was at the door"? "Nobody was out there."

"I must have been mistaken," he muttered to himself, closing the door, and making his way back to the fire. The group continued their conversation, but their unease was palpable.

Just as they started to relax again, another knock echoed through the cabin, but this time it came from the window in the back. Everyone jumped up. Kane and James quickly made their way to the back of the cabin to see what was causing the disturbance.

As they approached the window, James saw a dark figure darting into the forest. James quickly opened the window and stuck his head out, but the figure was nowhere in sight. He looked back at the group, shaking his head in confusion.

"It must have been a deer," he said, trying to ease the group's worries. But the group couldn't shake the feeling that something wasn't quite right.

James settled back into his seat by the fire. Kane, too returned to his chair by the fire. The atmosphere was tense, and everyone was on edge this time. The stories of Sasquatch from the Gitwinksihlkw men lingered in them. Suddenly, a loud bang hit the side of the cabin, sending everyone inside into a state of panic.

"What the hell was that?" Lisa cried out, clutching her chest.

"Everyone grab your flashlights and rifles," Tom shouted as he jumped up. Kane replied, "We need to go out and see what that was."

The men quickly followed Tom's lead, and they all went outside, shining their flashlights into the darkness. The first thing they saw was a huge tree leaning against the side of the cabin.

"What the hell?" James exclaimed as he approached the tree. "How did this even happen? Kane said, "It looks like it was ripped up out of the ground and thrown at the cabin."

"We need to check the surrounding area, and make sure there isn't anything else that could be out there," Tom instructed as he cautiously scanned the forest with his flashlight.

The men spread out, rifles at the ready, searching for any sign of what could have caused the tree to be thrown. But as they searched, they couldn't see anything out of the ordinary.

"I don't see anything," one of the Gitwinksihlkw men said as he returned to the group.

"Me neither," the others chimed in.

"We'll have to keep a watchful eye tonight, just in case," Tom said, leading the way back inside the cabin.

Tom: "Well, that was quite a scare. Everyone okay?"

Lisa: "Yeah, I think so. I just can't shake this feeling like something is out there and it is watching us."

Jenny: "I know what you mean. I'm going to have trouble sleeping tonight."

James: "Don't worry, it was probably just a branch falling from a tree. These woods can be dense, and it wouldn't be the first time I've seen something like that." Kane agreed to nod his head and said, "yea, probably a branch fell from the tree outside."

One of the men from Gitwinksihlkw: "I've been hunting in these woods for years, and I've heard of stories like this. Maybe we should keep watch tonight, just in case."

Tom: "I agree. We can take turns keeping watch. It's better to be safe than sorry."

James: "That's a good idea. I'll take the first shift."

Tom: "I'll take the second shift."

Kane: "I'll keep watch with you on the second shift too."

The men from Gitwinksihlkw: "We'll take the third and fourth shifts. Just wake us up when it's our turn."

Tom: "Sounds like a plan. Let's get some sleep. We have a big day ahead of us tomorrow."

As they all settled down, the cabin was filled with a sense of unease, but they knew they had each other's backs and would be okay. Despite the night's strange events, they were determined to find more evidence of Sasquatch and make the most of their time at the hunter's cabin.

The group grew tired as the night wore on, and they all retired to their rooms. James sat with his rifle while the others went to their bedrooms. Before they went to bed, Tom and Lisa discussed their plan for the next day, discussing the best areas to search.

With their minds filled with excitement and anticipation, Dr. Ross, Jenny, Tom, and Kane went to their rooms, then drifted off to sleep, dreaming of their search for Sasquatch. They were grateful for the unexpected company of James and the men from Gitwinksihlkw. James and the Gitwinksihlkw men had been keeping watch throughout the night for anything strange that might happen. They knew that their mission was critical and that they had to be alert at all times.

As the night went on, James began to feel a sense of unease. He couldn't shake the feeling that they were being watched. He tried to dismiss it as his imagination, but he couldn't ignore the hairs standing up on the back of his neck. He kept his rifle close at hand and remained vigilant.

Suddenly, he heard a strange noise coming from outside. It sounded like a deep growl, and it sent chills down his spine. He got up from his chair and peered out the window, but he couldn't see anything in the darkness.

He quietly made his way to the upstairs bedrooms where the others were sleeping, and woke them up. They could hear the growling too, and immediately jumped into action. James had his rifle ready. Tom and Kane armed themselves, and were ready to protect everyone in the cabin.

They cautiously stepped outside, and their worst fears were realized. Standing in the wooded forest in front of them was the massive creature, covered in dark hair, with piercing red eyes. It was Sasquatch, and it was angry. Tom, Kane, James and the three Gitwinksihlkw men stood frozen, unsure of what to do. The group stared at Sasquatch in shock and disbelief, unable to comprehend what they were seeing. Yet, here it was, standing before them, its massive form towering over them.

The creature let out another growl, this one even more menacing than the last. The group instinctively took a step back, but James stood his ground, his rifle aimed at the creature. The others looked at him in disbelief, wondering what he was planning to do.

James spoke softly, "Stay calm, everyone. We don't want to provoke it. Let's just back away slowly, and get back inside the cabin."

The group followed James' lead and started to retreat slowly. But as they stepped back, the Sasquatch suddenly charged toward them. James quickly fired a warning shot into the air, but it didn't stop the creature.

James, Tom, Kane, and the Gitwinksihlkw men barricaded the door. They could feel the creature pounding on the door, trying to break through. Meanwhile, Lisa and Jenny ran for their lives, trying to find a place to hide upstairs.

As they all caught their breath, they realized that they were in a dangerous situation. They knew that they had to devise a plan, and fast. But they also knew that they were no match for Sasquatch. All of a sudden, as fast as it started, it ended. They felt a sigh of relief as the tension between the creature and them ended. Sasquatch stopped his beating on the cabin door, and it had left them alone. You could feel the panic subside, and they all started to settle down, but the cabin was filled with a sense of unease, but they did have each other's back, and they would be okay, for now. Despite the night's strange events, they were determined to make the most of their time at the hunter's cabin.

Camera Seven

Tom, who was in charge of the cooking, whipped up a big breakfast for the men before they left. He wanted to ensure that they had an excellent meal to start the day, as he knew they would need all their strength and energy for the long journey ahead. The men sat down at the table and dug into their food, grateful for the hot meal that Tom had prepared for them.

After the men finished eating, Tom made breakfast for the rest of his group. He was a great cook who knew how to make the most of what they had. He fried some eggs and bacon, made some toast, and brewed a pot of coffee. The smell of the food woke Lisa and Jenny, eager to start their day after a good night's sleep.

They packed their gear, checked their weapons, and ensured everything was in order before they headed out. With a full stomach, and a sense of purpose, James, and the Gitwinksihlkw men stepped out of the cabin, and into the morning light. They set off on their journey, with their weapons at the ready, and their eyes peeled for any signs of danger. James: "Well, it's time for us to head back to the village. Thank you for your hospitality. We hope you find the evidence you seek. I appreciate your kindness." Tom: "It was our pleasure. We're glad you were here last night to help. Stay safe on your journey back."

Lisa: "Take care, and let us know if there's anything else we can do for your community." Jenny: "And don't be strangers. We will be here for a few more days. It would be great to have you men over again. The company was appreciated." James, "Thank you for the warm welcome.

It was great being here with all of you. I'll make sure to pass on the positive report about your operations here." Don: "We appreciate all the food and shelter. We'll be sure to come back and visit soon." John: "And thank you for showing us your hospitality." Gerald: "We'll see you again soon. Stay safe. The salmon feast was great. The scary entertainment was not, hahaha."

Lisa, Jenny, Tom, and Kane waved goodbye as James and the men headed out the door and started returning to Gitlaxt'aamiks. Kane said, "Keep your eyes open guys." "We will look for sure," James replied. Then they left, talking about last night's events. You could hear them in the distance, and then they were gone. Jenny checked the surveillance cameras at the trails. She was committed to ensuring the cameras were functioning correctly at all times. Lisa was behind Jenny, viewing the trail cam system. The computer and all 16 cameras displayed on the four screens. She was relieved that all cameras were functioning as they should, with no signs of wildlife. They could see the four men leave down the trail one after the other.

The camera feeds showed nothing but the trees swaying in the wind. This tranquil view helped Lisa to calm down, and she took a moment to appreciate the natural beauty of the surrounding forest.

Lisa and Jenny monitored the cameras closely but saw no further activity. She had recorded the incident from last night on the video cameras, and it was saved on the laptops. Then she made an entry into her notebook, but for now, she was content knowing that the cameras were functioning correctly and the trails were peaceful.

Tom was outside setting up his antenna for his ham radio equipment. Kane was helping him. After a bit, the cable was strung from the antenna and ran inside through the window. Kane was holding it outside and held onto it till Tom went into the cabin to take hold of it. Tom went inside, and over to the window, then reached for the cable. He plugged the end of the cable into his new FT-710 radio. He turned it on and pressed the tuner button on the radio. After it tuned the antenna, stations from around the world communicated with each other. Dr. Ross and Jenny were reviewing the footage from camera seven, which was set up on a remote trail in the wilderness. They were excited to see what kind of wildlife they could observe in the area. As they watched the footage, their attention was drawn to a movement in the brush. They zoomed in to get a better look and were shocked to see a large animal emerging from the trees. It had a sleek, deer-like form and moved gracefully along the trail.

"That's amazing!" Jenny exclaimed. "I've never seen a deer in real life before. They are so cute." Dr. Ross took a closer look at the animal and nodded. "It looks like a deer, but we'll have to examine the footage more closely. We don't want to jump to any conclusions."

As they continued to watch the footage, they noticed that the ham radio that Tom had set up in the cabin was making strange noises. It was filled with static, and they could hear bits of distant radio stations coming in and then fading out on the radio waves. It was a strange interference that they had never heard before.

Jenny looked up at Dr. Ross. "Do you think the radio interference could be related to the deer we saw on camera seven?"

Dr. Ross shook her head. "It's hard to say, but it's definitely worth investigating. Let's go see what Tom thinks."

They asked Tom, who was in the middle of a transmission on his ham radio. He was frowning as he tried to make sense of the static. "Tom, we saw a deer on camera seven," Dr. Ross said. "But we also noticed that the ham radio is making strange noises. Do you think there's any connection?"

Tom looked up from his radio and nodded. "It's possible. I've been experiencing this same interference for a few hours now. I've tried pinpointing the source but can't find it. It's frustrating."

Dr. Ross and Jenny exchanged a concerned look. They knew that Tom was an expert in his field, and if he couldn't figure out what was causing the interference, it was likely a serious problem. Kane even tried to help but didn't know much about Ham Radio.

"Maybe we should set up some more cameras in the area to see if we can observe any stranger behavior, and set up another monitor," Dr. Ross suggested. "And I think we should also watch the ham radio closely. If the interference is related to the deer, we saw on camera seven, it could be a significant discovery."

Tom agreed, and they set up additional cameras and monitored the ham radio. Over the next few hours, they observed more strange behavior from the deer, and the ham radio continued to experience interference. It was a mystery that they were determined to solve.

They gathered all of their data, and analyzed it carefully. They reviewed the footage from the cameras, the recordings from the ham radio, and any other observations they had made. It was a lot of information to sift through, but they were determined to find a connection.

Finally, after hours of intense analysis, they discovered the source of the strange behavior. The deer they had observed on camera seven was being watched from a distance. Dr. Ross and Jenny thought it might be a Sasquatch, but was well camouflaged. The creature's unique vocalizations caused the interference on the ham radio. It was a ground breaking discovery that would change the course of their research forever.

As Lisa and Jenny sat in the cabin monitoring the cameras, they saw something unexpected on camera five. It was a large black bear foraging for food in a nearby stream. The bear was massive and appeared to be searching for fish in the stream. Jenny couldn't help but marvel at its strength, and grace as it expertly navigated the rocky terrain.

As they continued to watch the bear, Lisa noticed movement on camera eight. She adjusted the focus and saw a pack of wolves moving through the forest, hunting for their next meal. The wolves were stealthy, and worked together as a team, communicating with each other as they searched for prey. Lisa and Jenny were both in awe of the wolves' cooperation and how they worked together to survive in the wild.

Suddenly, the ham radio crackled to life, interrupting their observations. A voice was breaking up, making determining what he was saying difficult. Tom was trying to get a better signal, but a wire antenna this close to the ground was the problem. But they could tell that he was trying to communicate an urgent message. They quickly turned their attention to the radio, trying to decipher what the man on the radio was trying to do.

Despite the interference, Tom was finally able to make out that a station in Germany was helping with emergency communications with another ham in Germany. The girls returned to their camera system, and there was an elk on camera eight, that was majestic, and towering, its antlers a symbol of its dominance in the forest. It was grazing on some grass, completely unaware of its surroundings. Lisa and Jenny were entranced by the elk's beauty, its peaceful presence a stark contrast to the wild animals they had just seen on the other cameras.

As they continued to watch the elk, Lisa heard movement outside the cabin. She cautiously approached the window and peered out, expecting to see Sasquatch. But instead, she saw a family of raccoons playing near the cabin. They were curious creatures, climbing the roof and scurrying around in the underbrush. Lisa couldn't help but smile at their playful antics, cute little faces, and bushy tails, making them hard to resist.

On camera nine, they saw a pair of foxes hunting in the nearby brush. The foxes were quick and agile, their bright red fur making them stand out against the green foliage. They worked together to track their prey, their movements graceful and synchronized. Lisa and Jenny were captivated by their hunting skills and how they worked together to get their food.

Meanwhile, the ham radio was still crackling with static, making it difficult for them to hear the audio from the trail cameras. But despite the interference, they continued to monitor the cameras, fascinated by the different animals they saw on their screens.

On camera eleven, they spotted a family of deer moving through the forest. The deer was delicate and graceful, their white tails a beacon and sensing danger. They were on the move, looking for food and water. Lisa and Jenny watched as the mother deer led her young through the brush, her instincts guiding her toward safety.

As they continued to observe the animals on the cameras, Lisa and Jenny were amazed at the diversity of life in the forest. They saw creatures they had never seen before and were fascinated by their different behaviors and habits. Despite their challenges, this was a once-in-a-lifetime opportunity to see so much wildlife up close and personal.

"Oh my god!" "What the hell!" Lisa said. Lisa and Jenny's hearts raced as they watched the footage on camera seven. They saw a significant, shadowy figure scoop up a deer with one hand and kill it effortlessly. The other deer scattered in fear, running in every direction to escape. The figure then walked away with the deer in its grip.

"Tom! Skyler! You have to come and see this!" Jenny yelled, trying to get their attention.

Tom and Skyler rushed into the cabin, curious about what was happening. As they approached the monitor, they saw the exact figure that Jenny and Lisa were horrified by.

"What the hell!" Tom blurted out, staring at the screen in disbelief. "Sasquatch has a deer in its hand!" Skyler blurted out.

"That is so sad," Jenny replied, her voice shaking. "But it just killed a deer with one hand."

Tom rubbed his chin, deep in thought. "I agree with Skyler. That is Sasquatch, and it is hunting for food. We have to go out there and see where it is going."

Jenny replied, "No Way in hell am I going out there." Lisa nodded in agreement. They were scared. They had never seen anything like this before and didn't know what to expect. "I will grab my rifle and go with you Tom," Skyler said.

Tom grabbed his binoculars and went outside, followed by Jenny and Lisa. Tom made his way toward the area where he saw the figure on the camera. Jenny and Lisa stayed behind. Skyler bolted out the door after Tom, catching up with him.

As he approached, he heard a rustling in the bushes. Suddenly, the figure stepped out into the open. It was a tall, humanoid creature with shaggy hair covering its body. It didn't smell very pleasant. "Oh, the stink!" Skyler said. " "yup smells horrible," Tom replied. Tom raised his binoculars to get a better look at the creature. "It's definitely Sasquatch," he whispered in amazement. Skyler replied, "with that stink, I would say it is a Sasquatch."

Jenny and Lisa were watching the camera feed and were speechless. The creature was giant and powerful and seemed aware of Tom and Skyler's presence, and then the creature turned its gaze toward Tom and Skyler. Jenny and Lisa felt their hearts racing. They didn't know what to do and were scared for their lives.

Tom stepped forward, trying to approach the creature. But as he did, it suddenly disappeared into the forest. Tom was left standing there. This Sasquatch was younger and far more dangerous than they had imagined. Despite the danger, Tom was determined to get more eyes on the creature.

He cautiously followed its trail, trying to get a better look at the creature. As Tom approached the area where the Sasquatch had disappeared, he noticed that the ground was heavily trampled and had broken branches everywhere. He could only imagine how strong the creature was to cause such destruction.

Meanwhile, in the cabin, Jenny and Lisa were still trying to process what they had just seen. They knew they had to tell someone about their discovery but feared what would happen if they did. They had been searching for Sasquatch, and had strong evidence now. They discussed the situation, and eventually, they decided to call their colleagues at the University.

Jenny and Lisa were determined to share the evidence they had uncovered with the scientific community. They contacted the Department Head | Professor Debra Maynard.

Lisa: "I've got some incredible news. We found proof, and we want to share it with you."

Debra: "Proof? That's amazing. Are you sure about this?"

Lisa: "Absolutely. We have video and audio recordings that we believe can provide valuable insight into the existence of Sasquatch, and prove this new hominid indeed exists."

Debra: "This is remarkable. Please send us the footage via the satellite link at your cabin, and we'll get back to you as soon as we've had a chance to review it."

Jenny compiled the data and sent it to Professor Maynard, eagerly awaiting their response.

Meanwhile, Tom and Skyler continued to follow the trail of the Sasquatch, amazed by its strength and power. As they got closer to where it had disappeared into the forest, he noticed the ground becoming softer and muddier, making the trail harder to follow. However, Tom remained determined to track this elusive creature and pressed on, knowing that this might be his only chance to see it again. Skyler, he was there for Toms' backup. Just in case things went south.

In the cabin, Jenny and Lisa were increasingly worried about Tom and Skyler out there chasing a Sasquatch. They knew they needed to get this footage about their discovery back to UBC, but they also knew they needed to be careful. They had sent some footage of the incident and were waiting on UBC, and they were afraid that if they told the wrong people, their evidence would be destroyed or covered up. They tried to devise a plan, but their nerves were getting the best of them.

Finally, Tom and Skyler emerged from the forest. Jenny and Lisa were relieved to see them back on the camera. They rushed to meet them, eager to hear what they saw. "I saw it," Tom said, his voice shaking. "It was incredible. Skyler added, "It stunk to high heavens." Tom continued, "It was so big, and it was walking on two legs. I've never seen anything like it that close to me." Jenny and Lisa listened in amazement as Tom told them what he had seen, and they couldn't believe they had finally found concrete evidence of Sasquatch. They informed Tom that they managed to get the footage to the University of British Columbia, where it could be shared with experts in the field.

Jenny and Skyler Gather Firewood

Jenny and Skyler walked into the forest to gather firewood for the cabin. As they walked, Skyler pointed out different types of trees and explained their uses. Jenny was fascinated by his knowledge and asked him about his experience in the wilderness.

"I've spent a lot of time in the wilderness over the years," Kane said. "It's important to know how to survive in these conditions, not just for your own safety, but for the safety of others." As they were collecting firewood, Skyler and Jenny came across a lookout at the mountains. They decided to take a break and sat down to admire the view. Jenny snapped pictures for a while. She couldn't help but notice how handsome and rugged Skyler looked, and she found herself becoming infatuated with him.

"This is such a beautiful view," she said, trying to hide her attraction. "I'm glad we came out here to collect firewood."

Skyler turned to her and smiled. "I'm glad too," he said. "It's always nice to take a break and appreciate the beauty of nature."

As they sat there, Jenny's infatuation with Officer Kane became increasingly obvious. She found herself staring into his eyes, and he seemed to be doing the same. Without warning, Officer Kane moved in, and they shared a long, passionate kiss. They embraced and kissed more deeply, lost in the moment.

The two of them were so caught up in the moment that they didn't hear the sound of twigs snapping and footsteps approaching. They were interrupted by Lisa and Tom returning from the hike. Jenny and Skyler broke apart, feeling embarrassed but happy with what had just happened.

Lisa and Tom were out getting firewood too and were on their way back to the cabin when they stumbled upon Jenny and Skyler. They found the two of them embraced in a passionate kiss.

Lisa and Tom were taken aback by what they saw. They quickly realized that they had interrupted a private moment and apologized. "We're so sorry," Lisa said. "We didn't mean to interrupt."

Jenny and Kane both looked embarrassed and a bit flustered. They quickly composed themselves and tried to play it off as if nothing had happened. "It's okay," Skyler said. "We were just taking a break and enjoying the view."

Lisa and Tom looked at the view. Lisa took a few pictures; however, they could tell that there was something more going on between Jenny and Skyler. They didn't want to pry, but they could see that there was definitely a spark between the two of them.

The group quickly changed the subject and continued their discussion about the hike to the Tseax cone tomorrow. However, Lisa and Tom couldn't help but feel curious about the connection between Jenny and Officer Kane. They didn't know what to expect, but they were excited to see how things would develop between them.

With the firewood collected, the group of four set off back to the cabin. They walked through the forest, chatting and laughing, enjoying each other's company. Officer Kane took the lead, guiding them through the dense forest, and pointing out potential hazards and areas of interest.

As they walked, Lisa and Tom couldn't help but notice the way Jenny and Officer Kane were interacting. They seemed more relaxed and comfortable with each other, and there was a certain chemistry between them.

Jenny and Officer Kane, on the other hand, were trying to keep their feelings for each other in check. They had been caught up in the moment earlier.

The group returned to the cabin and started a fire in the wood stove and was getting ready to cook dinner. As the night went on, they grew tired and decided to call it a night. Jenny walked to her room, and Skyler went to his room. With several knocks on Skyler's door, he got up and out of bed. It was Jenny. "Can I come in?" "Of course, you can come in, Jenny."

Jenny and Skyler sat on the bed talking, and they couldn't help but think about the kiss they had shared earlier. They both felt a strong attraction to each other and were finding it hard to resist. They couldn't help but steal glances at each other as they sat and talked. The tension between them was palpable. They started to speak softly, and their conversation soon turned into flirting.

Skyler reached out and touched Jenny's face, and she leaned into his touch. They kissed softly at first, and then their kisses became more passionate. They explored each other's bodies with their hands, feeling a strong connection between them. Jenny and Skyler gave into their attraction and shared more passionate kisses.

They explored each other's bodies, feeling the intense chemistry between them. As their desire grew, they removed each other's clothes with urgency, eager to feel each other's touch. Jenny took the lead, climbing on top of Skyler, and they moved together in a natural and perfect rhythm.

They enjoyed each other's touch, relishing in the intense pleasure they created. Skyler then moved behind Jenny, and their bodies moved in sync, reaching new heights of ecstasy. They were lost in the moment, wrapped up in each other's embrace, and savored every touch and kiss. They both experienced intense pleasure together, reaching their peak in unison.

Jenny and Officer Kane were both happy and content, but at the same time, they were a bit nervous about how things would be between them. They both knew that their relationship would change the dynamics of the group, but they were willing to take that risk.

Jenny and Skyler lay in each other's arms, their breathing slowly returning to normal. The only sounds in the room were their soft whispers and the gentle rustling of sheets as they cuddled together. They gazed into each other's eyes, smiling and feeling the warmth of their intimacy. As they lay there, Jenny felt a wave of emotion wash over her. She had never felt so close to anyone before, and the intensity of their lovemaking had only strengthened that feeling. Jenny was looking forward to the next adventure together.

Skyler sensed her emotions and held her tightly, knowing that she needed his comfort. "Are you okay?" he asked, his voice filled with concern. Jenny smiled up at him, feeling safe and secure in his arms. "I'm more than okay," she replied. "That was incredible." Skyler grinned, feeling proud of their shared experience. "You were amazing," he said. "I couldn't have done it without you." They both laughed, feeling the joy and connection that comes from sharing something so intimate with another person.

They continued to hold each other, basking in the afterglow of their lovemaking. As they lay there, Jenny realized that this was just the beginning of their journey together. She knew that they had something special, and she couldn't wait to see what the future held. Skyler felt the same way, knowing that their passion was only going to deepen as they continued to explore each other.

Kidnapped By Sasquatch

The next morning, the group woke up, and there was a different vibe in the air. Lisa and Tom could tell that something had changed between Jenny and Officer Kane. They decided not to say anything and let things develop naturally between them.

The group cooked breakfast as Jenny and Skyler were smiling, then they grabbed their backpacks and firearms then set off on their journey to the Tseax. Jenny and Officer Kane walked together, their hands intertwined, both of them smiling and happy. As they walked through the forest, the group couldn't help but feel like they were being watched. They noticed that the trees around them were snapped, broken, and hanging 6 feet up, pointing in the direction they were coming from. Tom, who had been leading the group, said, "That's really weird. I've never seen anything like this before." The group looked around nervously, trying to shake the feeling that they were being followed.

The journey took a stranger turn when they came across four trees that were completely upside down. The trees were pulled out of the ground and pushed back into the ground, the roots were pointing up toward the sky. The group couldn't understand how such a thing was possible, and they were left feeling disoriented and confused. They looked around, trying to find an explanation for the bizarre sight, but they couldn't find any.

Jenny exchanged worried glances, wondering if they should turn back or continue on. "Do you think it's safe to continue?" Jenny asked. "I don't know, but we should be careful," Officer Kane replied, tightening his grip on his firearm. Tom gripped his shotgun to the ready and said "keep your eyes peeled" The group moved on, keeping a close eye on their surroundings, and trying to stay alert for any potential dangers.

Despite their unease, the group pressed on, determined to reach their destination. They were on a mission, and the Tseax was not too far away. They just had to keep their wits about them and be ready for anything. As they were making their way through the dense forest, they came across another peculiar sight, they approached a tee-pee structure, and they heard noises coming from the surrounding area. They examined the Four trees that had been put together in the shape of a tee-pee; the branches were interwoven at the top to create a structure that seemed out of place in the natural environment. The group was intrigued by this structure and wondered who or what could have built it and for what purpose. Inside there were leaves and tree branches and it seemed to be a place to sleep. A foul smell was emitting from inside, there was a lot of hair in and around the structure.

They knew that this was not a natural occurrence and that it could be a sign that Sasquatch might have made this to sleep in. The activity in the area certainty pointed to Sasquatch.

They continued to hear Branches breaking, and the sound of rustling leaves could be heard. The group was on high alert, knowing that the noises could be caused by wildlife or something else. They moved cautiously, keeping their eyes and ears open for any signs of danger. The group was on high alert, wondering if they were about to encounter something dangerous. Suddenly, a Nisga'a man emerged from the trees, catching the group by surprise. The man appeared in his mid-sixties, with weathered skin and deep lines etched on his face. He was wearing traditional clothing, including a woven cedar hat and a button blanket.

The Nisga'a man said ṅit to the group in his language, and Officer Kane, who spoke some of the language replied ṅit back. Officer Kane said Lisa, Jenny and Tom had been sent to the remote area to investigate reports of strange noises and disturbances that had been heard in the region. It was said that the sounds were coming from Sasquatch that lived in the dense forest. But, this time they found the source of this noise. The Nisga'a man introduced himself as Gwiix-siiliṅskw, a renowned hunter.

The team was both surprised and relieved to find that the man was friendly. They had heard many tales of the Nisga'a people and their mystical connection to the land. Gwiix-siiliṅskw explained that he was a skilled hunter and that the noises the team had heard were from his hunting activities. He was trapping some animals in the area and using traditional Nisga'a methods that involved using noise to drive the animals to him. He also mentioned that there was a nearby village where they could find more information about the area.

Officer Kane and his team were intrigued by the man's story and wanted to know more about the village. They asked him if he could take them there, and he agreed, saying that he would be happy to guide them.

As they walked, Gwiix-siiliṅskw shared stories of the Nisga'a people and their culture. He talked about their deep connection to the land, their customs, and their way of life. The team was fascinated by his words and felt honored to be in his presence.

After a while, they arrived at the village, which was a small settlement of wooden longhouses. The team was greeted by a group of friendly villagers who welcomed them and invited them to take a tour of their village. Officer Kane and his team were amazed by what they saw. The village had cedar longhouses and was built entirely from natural resources, and the people were self-sufficient, growing their food and hunting for their meat.

The team was especially impressed by the people's respect for nature and their traditional way of life. They learned more about the Nisga'a culture, their music, and their art. They were fascinated by the intricate carvings and weaving that the people made from natural materials.

As the day went on, Officer Kane and his team were invited to a traditional Nisga'a feast. They were served a delicious meal of smoked salmon, venison, and other local delicacies. They were also treated to a dance performance that was both beautiful and mesmerizing.

Lisa and Jenny felt privileged to have been a part of the Nisga'a community for a day. They had learned so much more about the people and their culture, and they felt a deep sense of respect and admiration for the Nisga'a way of life.

As they prepared to leave, Gwiix-siilinskw approached Officer Kane and thanked him and his group for being respectful and understanding of the Nisga'a way of life. He said that he hoped they would take the lessons they had learned with them and share them with others.

Lisa, Jenny and Tom along with Officer Kane taking up the rear of the group, left the village with a newfound appreciation for the land and the people who lived on it. They knew that they had been given a unique opportunity to learn about a culture that was both ancient and vibrant.

The group was excited to see the Tseax up close and personal. As they arrived at the outer area of the volcano, they could see the vegetation, and some smoke was rising from the crater. They geared up and began their hike around the cinder cone volcano. The trail was rugged and steep, but the group was determined to reach the center of the cone.

The group spent the next few hours hiking around the volcano and taking pictures, and soaking in all of the sights and sounds. Once they reached the center, the group spent the next few hours resting and cooking food on their gas stoves.

Jenny was starting to see Lisa look and feel discouraged and frustrated. Dr. Ross, who had been leading the research, was starting to feel the pressure. She was worried about the funding for the project, as she had invested a lot of her own money into the research. She was also worried about what the scientific community would think if they wouldn't accept the evidence of Sasquatch's existence. The mood was tense, and there was a palpable feeling of disappointment in the air. Tom, Jenny, and Officer Kane were all trying to keep up a positive attitude, but they were seeing Lisa starting to lose hope. It was all over her face.

The group packed up and started hiking back on the trail toward the hunters cabin. They continued to move forward cautiously, their nerves on edge. They reached another small clearing, and they were not prepared to see what they saw when they got there.. They were horrified to see several deer carcasses scattered around the area. The animals had clearly been killed by something or someone, and they all felt a shiver run down their spine. "This is senseless killing, not for food at all," Tom stated.

Jenny went behind a tree and was about to throw up, the carcasses smelled bad, and she was becoming nauseous. Then all of a sudden she did start throwing up. Lisa and Tom could hear her throwing up behind the tree.

Then the group heard a blood curdling scream. Jenny started yelling and screaming as she was picked up by Sasquatch, he gripped her tightly and she was crying and in pain from the grip. Tom looked back to the tree Jenny was standing behind. It was then that they realized that Jenny had been taken by Sasquatch. The group then saw the flash of Sasquatch with Jenny over its shoulder leaving the area at a fast pace. Then, it was gone out of their sight while Jenny was yelling for help. They could hear her crying in agony, the screaming continued till they couldn't hear her anymore. "Oh no, do you think she is still alive? I can't hear her anymore." Dr. Ross said as tears rolled down her face. Officer Kane replied, "I don't know. This is crazy, really fucking crazy." "It left a lot of tracks to follow, plus the stink of it will be easier to follow." Tom blurted out.

As the Sasquatch made its way deeper into the forest, the rest of the group was in a state of shock. They couldn't hear Jenny's screams echoing through the trees anymore, and they knew this was bad, and they had to act quickly to save her. Tom, Dr. Ross, and Officer Kane quickly gathered their equipment and set out in pursuit of the Sasquatch. They knew the forest was dangerous, and they needed to be careful, but they were determined to save Jenny.

As they ran through the dense forest, they could hear Jenny's screams emerging in the air, but it was getting weaker and weaker. They feared that the Sasquatch might be hurting her, and they pushed themselves to move faster. Tom was in the lead, using his knowledge of the area to navigate through the trees. Dr. Ross and Officer Kane followed behind, keeping their eyes open for any sign of the Sasquatch's prints. Finally, they reached a small clearing, and they could see the Sasquatch in the distance, with Jenny thrown over his shoulder. Officer Kane raised his rifle, and looked through the scope, there was no shot. It would have hit Jenny.

They approached cautiously, not wanting to startle the creature and make a tense situation more dangerous. But as they got closer, the Sasquatch suddenly turned and faced them and growled. Kane had his chance; a shot was open to the taking. Just as he was ready to squeeze the trigger, the Sasquatch moved and this put Jenny back into the shot.

The group could see the fear in Jenny's eyes, and they knew that they had to act quickly to save her. Tom stepped forward knelt down and opened his arms for the creature to release her into his arms like you would do with your dog, you know to get the ball back. "Let her go. Hey! Please let her go, we need her back with us. You don't need her." The Sasquatch grunted as if to say no. He spoke softly, trying to calm the creature. "We are not here to hurt you. We only want to know about you. That's all." But the Sasquatch seemed agitated, and it began to pace back and forth, growling. The group was feeling a sense of dread, the fear was almost too much for them. Lisa was still crying, and Jenny could see the pain in Lisa's face as she herself was crying. Jenny said, "I love you, Lisa." "I love you too Jenny." "it's going to be all right, we'll get you out of this situation. I promise you we will." 'I know you will." Lisa and Officer Kane stepped forward, trying to help Tom. They tried to talk to the Sasquatch, but it wouldn't listen. They could see that the creature was getting more and more agitated, and they feared that it might attack at any moment.

As the tension rose, the Sasquatch suddenly let out a loud roar and lunged forward. The group scattered, trying to get out of the way. Jenny got up and tried to run. But the Sasquatch grabbed her again; it was too quick, and then it tightened its grip on Jenny and ran back into the forest, with Jenny screaming and crying. The rest of the group regrouped and continued their pursuit, but they could hear the Sasquatch getting further and further away.

They were heartbroken, knowing that they were losing Jenny. They pushed themselves to move faster, knowing that every second counted. They were determined to save her, no matter what it took. A few minutes later they couldn't hear Jenny or Sasquatch. They strained to listen, but nothing was heard, only the pounding of their hearts in their throats.

Kane and Tom tracked the path the creature left in its wake. It went up the mountain toward the hunter's cabin, and they followed that track. The smell was in the air and Kane and Lisa felt nauseous. They thought poor Jenny, being right with it, must be making her sick. Tom lost track. Kane picked it up, heading eastward toward the Tseax.

But as the hours passed, they began to fear that they would never find her. They searched through the night, but they couldn't find any sign of the Sasquatch or Jenny. They were exhausted and discouraged, but they refused to give up.

They knew they had to keep searching, no matter how difficult it was. As they continued their search, they encountered many obstacles and challenges. They had to cross a river and climb over fallen trees, but they pushed on, determined to find Jenny. Finally, after what felt like an eternity, they heard Jenny's cries for help.

As they ran, Tom's thoughts raced. He was filled with fear for Jenny's safety, but also a sense of determination to rescue her. He had come on this expedition hoping to find evidence of Sasquatch's existence, but he never expected to be in a situation like this.

Dr. Ross was also filled with fear, but she tried to stay focused on the task at hand. She knew that they needed to get Jenny as quickly as possible and make sure she was safe. She stopped to catch her breath, then broke down crying. Officer Kane hugged Lisa. "We'll find her, I promise Lisa, we'll find her." Sasquatch had surprised them all, but they couldn't give up now.

Sasquatch put Jenny on the ground He looked at her, crying and curled up on the floor and groaning, but that grumble sounded like a nervous grunt. She looked up at him, then a voice said in her head, "leave my house, leave us alone" and then she saw an image of her and the group leaving through the trees and driving off in their truck. Did this creature just get into her brain somehow? Can Sasquatch communicate telepathically? Jenny looked around and realized she was in a large cave. Sasquatch communicated "my home, leave my home"

Jenny was bewildered as to what was going on. This cave had an opening at the top and the sun shined into it to light the cave up. She was on the ground next to a tree growing in the cave. Jenny was amazed at the size of this cave. She had never experienced anything like this before, and she didn't know if she could find her way out. But she was certain of one thing: the voice she heard was not hers. There was another image of her quickly packing up her things and the others starting back on the trail to leave, again, a voice followed the images "You have to leave the forest and never come back. If you do, you will face more serious consequences."

Jenny could sense the urgency and seriousness in the image of the creature that was projected into her head. She realized that there are some things in this world that are beyond human understanding, and this is one. She wanted to respect his wish to be alone. But she had no clue how to leave the cave. Jenny was trapped with the beast, completely at its mercy. The Sasquatch communicated again with her through telepathy, telling her of its plans for her. She was scared out of her mind, not knowing what was happening to her. She could feel its anger and its hunger, and she knew she was in grave danger.

She heard a voice in her mind once more. The voice said, "I need your help."

Jenny was shocked. She asked, "What can I do for you?"

Sasquatch replied, "The forest is in danger. Humans are destroying our homes and killing our food. Poachers killed our deer. We need you to spread the word and help us protect our home."

Jenny agreed to help. She knew no one would believe her if she told them about her telepathic conversation with Sasquatch, so she was going to keep it a secret. Meanwhile, Tom, Dr. Lisa, and Officer Kane were searching the forest for Jenny. They were worried because she had been gone for hours and they feared the worst.

As they searched, they stumbled upon some of the creature's footprints again. Dr. Lisa said, "We're getting close." Officer Kane said, "We need to find Jenny as soon as possible. We don't want her death on our conscience, I love that girl." That statement resonated with Tom and Lisa. Their relationship started not that long ago, and now he is so involved with her. Then the footprints disappeared bringing a sense of despair. The group came to a rock face with outcroppings of trees. They searched the ground for more footprints, but there were none. "They couldn't just disappear just like that?" Tom said. "No, there must be some way into this rock structure. Keep searching; there has to be an entrance," replied Kane.

They finally stumbled upon an entrance to the cave. In a desperate attempt to save Jenny, the search party entered the cave, armed with only their courage and their faith. Just then, they heard a voice calling for help. It was Jenny! They rushed to her and found her sitting against a tree, shaking, crying and in shock. Dr. Ross grabbed her med kit from her pack. Took out a syringe, tip, and a bottle of dopamine. Lisa's hands were shaking as she put the needle tip on the syringe. The needle was pushed through the protector of the bottle, and she filled it to 40 mg/mL. "Ok, ok, ok, just a little pinprick, there'll be no more, ah, but you may feel a little sick... There you go, just relax" Dr. Ross said. Jenny was sedated in seconds.

When they asked her what had happened. Jenny told them "I had a telepathic conversation with Sasquatch. He asked me to help protect the Sasquatch females and children, the forest, and their food supply from the humans." "He telepathically showed me the way to get out of the cave." The others were stunned. They trusted Jenny, but this was strange, to say the least. But officer Kane picked her up into his arms to help her get out of that cave and back to the Cabin. It was evident he wanted to get her warmed up by the fire and get her water and food.

White Light In The Sky

Tom stepped outside of cabin, adjusting his glasses as he gazed up at the sky. He had been tinkering with his ham radio for hours, trying to get the reception just right. As he reached up to adjust the antenna, he suddenly felt a strange sensation, like a weightlessness pulling him upward. Before he could react, he was engulfed in a blinding white light.

Inside the cabin, Lisa, Jenny, and Skyler were gathered around the table, chatting idly. As the white light flooded the window, they all jumped to their feet, their hearts racing with fear and confusion. They rushed outside, calling out to Tom, trying to make sense of the bizarre scene unfolding before them.

"Tom! Tom, what's happening?!" Lisa shouted, cupping her hands around her mouth.

But it was too late. Tom was lifted off the ground, his body disappearing into the heart of the light. The girls were frozen in place, stunned and bewildered by what they had just witnessed.

As the light faded and the ship began to move away, Lisa, Jenny, and Skyler were left standing in the dark, staring up at the stars in shock. They knew they had to do something, but they didn't know where to start.

After a few moments of silence, Skyler sprang into action, grabbing the satellite phone and dialing the police department's emergency number. He explained the situation to the dispatcher, his voice trembling with fear and anxiety.

Within minutes, a team of search and rescue professionals had been dispatched from Terrace to the cabin. The group were racing against time to find Tom and bring him back to safety. The police arrived an hour thereafter, their flashing lights casting an eerie glow over the remote wilderness.

As they waited anxiously for news, Lisa, Jenny, and Skyler huddled together, their minds racing with questions and doubts. What had just happened? Where had Tom gone? And most importantly, would he ever return?

The search and rescue team arrived two hours later and scoured the area around the cabin for any clues or evidence of what might have happened. They combed the woods, searched nearby lakes and streams, and even used helicopters to scan the surrounding hillsides. But despite their best efforts, they found nothing.

The police, meanwhile, interviewed the girls, trying to piece together what had happened in the moments leading up to Tom's disappearance. Lisa, Jenny, and Skyler recounted their version of events, describing the blinding light and the sudden lift-off that had taken Tom from their midst.

As the hours passed, the search and rescue team grew increasingly concerned. The weather was starting to turn, with a cold rain beginning to fall from the sky. They knew that time was running out.

But just as it seemed that all hope was lost, they received a radio transmission from a group of hikers who had been exploring the nearby hills. They had seen a strange object hovering in the sky, and had managed to capture a video of it on their cell phones.

The police and search and rescue teams rushed to the coordinates given by the hikers, and were amazed to find a large, metallic craft hovering silently in the air. They cautiously approached the object, their guns drawn and ready for anything.

As the team drew closer to the craft, they could see that it was unlike anything they had ever seen before. It was massive, easily the size of a small house, and seemed to be made of some kind of sleek, metallic material. There were no visible markings or identifying features on the craft, and it seemed to be completely silent.

As they circled the craft, searching for any signs of life or movement, they noticed a small door on the side of the craft slowly sliding open. Everyone tensed up, their guns at the ready, as they waited to see what would emerge.

But to their surprise, the first thing that stepped out of the craft was not an alien or an otherworldly creature, but a human-like figure clad in a strange, metallic suit. The figure held up its hands in a gesture of surrender, and spoke in a strange, garbled language that nobody could understand.

The team cautiously approached the figure, their guns still at the ready, but the figure did not seem to pose any immediate threat. As they got closer, they could see that the suit was intricately designed, with glowing lights and strange, pulsing symbols etched into the surface.

After a few moments of tense negotiation, the figure managed to convey that it was not a threat, but was simply a scout from an advanced alien civilization. They had been observing Earth for centuries, the figure explained, and had been fascinated by humanity's progress and potential.

Tom was completely disoriented as he regained consciousness. He found himself lying on a cold, metallic surface, surrounded by the dim, otherworldly glow of the alien spacecraft. His head was pounding, and he could barely remember how he had gotten there.

Slowly, he became aware of the two reptilian aliens standing before him, their piercing gaze fixed on him. He tried to move, but found that he was completely paralyzed, unable to even twitch a muscle.

"Welcome, Tom," one of the reptilians hissed. "We are pleased to have you with us."

Tom's heart pounded in his chest as he struggled to make sense of what was happening. The last thing he remembered was stepping outside to tune his ham radio antenna, and now he was onboard an alien spacecraft, completely at the mercy of these bizarre, otherworldly creatures.

As he watched, the two Grey aliens who seemed to be in control of the ship approached him. They began to communicate with the reptilians in a strange, guttural language that Tom couldn't understand.

But then, something strange began to happen. Tom felt a strange, warm sensation filling his mind, like a soft, soothing voice whispering in his ear. He realized that two Sasquatch aliens teleported next to him and were communicating with him telepathically.

Their words filled his mind, telling him about the two different kinds of Sasquatch. One group was a spiritual being, much like humans, that accessed the earth through portals. The other group was a subset of human Sasquatch hybrids that had been created over 100,000 years ago. These hybrids had been living alone in pod families and wanted nothing to do with humans. They feared humans because of the destruction of their homes from deforestation and over-hunting of their food supply, and the active hunting of them and their children.

Tom felt a sense of sadness and despair as he realized the damage that humans had inflicted upon these creatures. The Sasquatch aliens warned him that if humans didn't change their ways and stop destroying the earth with wars and advanced weapons, it would lead to nuclear war and the end of everything, including both humans and the Sasquatch species.

As the message faded away, Tom was left feeling stunned and bewildered. He had just received a warning from beings that he had never even known existed, and he had no idea what to do with this newfound knowledge.

Tom's mind was racing as he listened to the Sasquatch aliens. He couldn't believe what he was hearing. He had always been fascinated by Sasquatch sightings and stories, but he never thought he would actually encounter them in such an otherworldly setting.

The Sasquatch aliens continued to explain to Tom that they had been monitoring Earth for centuries, and they had seen the damage that humans had inflicted on the planet. They were afraid that humans would eventually destroy everything, including themselves and the Sasquatch species. They had been working with the aliens on the spacecraft to try and find a way to stop this from happening.

Tom asked the Sasquatch aliens what he could do to help. They told him that he had been chosen for a special mission. He was to be sent back to Earth as a messenger, to share the Sasquatch's message with humanity.

Tom was overwhelmed by the enormity of the task. He asked the aliens how he could possibly convince people to change their ways and save the planet. The Sasquatch aliens told him that he would be given a special gift, a unique perspective that would help people to see the world in a new way.

As Tom pondered his mission, he suddenly felt a jolt. The spacecraft was descending rapidly. The Sasquatch aliens told him that he needed to prepare himself, as he would soon be back on Earth and his mission would begin. Tom took a deep breath, ready to face whatever was ahead of him.

As the spacecraft descended towards the ground, Tom felt a strange sensation in his head. It was as if his brain had suddenly come alive, firing on all cylinders. He realized that the reptilians had implanted a chip in his brain, activating his mind to its full capacity.

Tom was astonished by what he was able to see and understand. He had access to all of the advanced communications, computers, and brain implants that the humans of Earth would be able to develop. He saw blueprints for advanced technologies that could revolutionize the world as we know it.

The reptilians began to explain to Tom how these technologies worked. They showed him how to create Nano-Robots that could mine minerals for spacecraft production, using protective metals and advanced propulsion systems. They even showed him how to make the craft repairable, invisible, and capable of teleportation to other sectors of space.

Tom was overwhelmed by the vastness of the knowledge he was being given. The reptilians also shared with him details about gene editing that could cure all diseases, extend human life expectancy, and even ways to grow food to feed the world's population.

As Tom absorbed all of this information, he also learned about unlimited energy sources that could power the world without harming the environment. He saw visions of a brighter future for humanity, where all people would be free from the struggles and limitations that currently hold them back.

Tom knew that he had been given a gift, and he had a responsibility to share it with the world. As the spacecraft hovered above Earth, he prepared himself for the mission that lay ahead. He would use his newfound knowledge to make a difference and change the world for the better.

As the light appeared from the sky, Lisa, Jenny, Skyler, and the search and rescue team watched in amazement as Tom descended from the spaceship. The police officers were astounded by what they were seeing, and Skyler's story was now corroborated. Tom was returned to Earth, back at the cabin, ten hours after he had disappeared. The police approached him, asking him what had happened, but Tom had an unreal story and withheld information for his own safety.

After his health was checked by the search and rescue team, Tom was cleared to go. The police left the scene and returned to their detachment, while the search and rescue team headed back to Terrace.

Lisa, Jenny, and Skyler stood in stunned silence as Tom shared the incredible technology and knowledge he had been implanted with on the alien spacecraft. They couldn't believe what they were seeing and hearing. As the holographic screen flickered in mid-air, Tom played the recording of the Sasquatch alien's mind speak, explaining the dire consequences of humanity's destructive behavior.

After Tom finished sharing the information, a look of worry crossed his face. "I can't tell anyone about this," he said. "I don't know who to trust. The wrong people finding out about this could mean my life is in danger."

Lisa, Jenny, and Skyler exchanged uneasy glances. They knew the importance of keeping this information a secret. They pledged to protect Tom and the knowledge he had been given, no matter what.

Then Tom, Lisa, Jenny, and Skyler huddled together, discussing the implications of what they had learned. They knew that the information Tom had shared with them was not something they could just tell anyone. The advanced technology, medical breakthroughs, and unlimited energy could change the world, but it could also fall into the wrong hands.

As they talked, they came up with a plan. They would reach out to scientists, engineers, and other experts who they trusted to work on these projects in secret. They would form a team, working towards a brighter future for humanity while keeping their discoveries hidden from those who would use it for evil.

They also knew that they had to protect Tom. The aliens who had implanted the chip in his brain could come looking for him at any moment, and they had no way of knowing if they were friendly or not. Not only that. They had to worry about the government knowing and taking Tom and gaining this information from him, in nefarious ways. They agreed to keep Tom's whereabouts a secret. He would stay at his home till Lisa and Jenny formed this scientific group at UBC.

The group had spent the night discussing their plans and making sure they had everything they needed for their journey back to the Lava Beds where Tom's truck was parked. They had agreed to leave the cabin the next day, as soon as the sun rose, and head back to civilization.

Keep Our Secret

As the day began to wind down, they packed all their audio and trail cameras laptops and radio equipment then the group made their descent. Though exhausted, they needed to tell their story and about their experience. The descent was not without its challenges, as the group had to navigate through the trail back down to base camp. It was getting dark, and it started to rain. They had to be cautious and take their time to ensure they didn't slip or fall. The trail was steep and slippery, but the group was focused on getting back safely.

As they approached the tepee structure, the group felt a sense of unease wash over them again. The memories of their previous encounter with the mysterious structure and the unknown noises in the surrounding area are still fresh in their minds. They heard branches breaking, and the sound of rustling leaves, and their hearts began to race. "Do you think it's safe to go back?" Jenny whispered, her voice trembling. "We are armed. Anything that attacks us won't do good," Kane replied, tightening his grip on his firearm.

Tom, gripping his shotgun, said, "I wonder if it is the same guy we saw before. Maybe he is camped out here." The group moved on, trying to stay alert and keep a close eye on their surroundings. They were determined to reach their destination, but the thought of encountering something dangerous made them uneasy.

As they got closer to the tepee structure, they saw a pair of glowing eyes staring at them from the trees. The group froze, unsure of what to do. Suddenly, a loud scream echoed through the forest. The group became terrified, uncertain if the creature would attack them. But to their surprise, it didn't attack. It simply stood there, staring at them.

Jenny, who had been frozen with fear, finally found her voice and asked, "What do we do? I don't want this thing to take me again " Officer Kane replied, "I won't let that happen again Jenny. We need to keep calm and not make sudden movements. We don't want to provoke it." The group slowly backed away, keeping watch on the glowing eyes staring back at them.

They backed away and slowly descended down the trail, Jenny thought about encountering another one of these creatures, and that weighed heavy on her mind. She couldn't shake the feeling that she was being watched, and Jenny knew she needed to be extra careful as she made her way back to Toms truck.

Then they heard a loud series of knocking on a tree, followed by a strange whoop from outside. The group froze, their eyes wide with fear. "oh no, no, no it followed us!" Jenny cried out, her voice shaking. "It sounds like it is trying to scare us away," said Lisa. "it's working. I'm thoroughly scared," Jenny said.

They were on high alert as they heard more tree knocks from the surrounding forest. They were unsure what to make of it, but they knew the noise was getting closer to them. The group exchanged worried glances, uncertain of what to do next.

Suddenly, the whooping that they had heard before increased in volume and intensity, and it was clear that there was more than one creature. The group realized that they were not alone in this forest, and that there were multiple Sasquatch in the area. They were terrified by this realization.

Then Jenny tried to communicate back with the Sasquatch, using the same telepathy as before. They were not hearing any whooping now. Jenny was surprised when the Sasquatch responded, and the telepathy changed in tone and rhythm. The group started to receive the messages now and were amazed that they could communicate with the creatures through their minds. They began to feel a sense of connection with them. However, they needed to figure out what they were saying.

Lisa: "I can't believe we're communicating with Sasquatch. What do you think it's trying to say?" Jenny: "It sounds like it's trying to communicate something more complex. Listen, it's changing the tone and rhythm of the thought it's making."

Skyler: "Yeah, it's almost like it's trying to convey different words or phrases. It's like it's trying to tell us something specific."

Lisa: "Maybe it's trying to tell us about itself or its habitat. Or maybe it's trying to tell us about other Sasquatch in the area."

Tom: "It's hard to say for sure, but whatever it's trying to say, it's clear that it's intelligent and capable of communication."

The group continued to listen and communicate with the Sasquatch, trying to understand what it was trying to say. They listened carefully to the sounds and tones to identify patterns or meanings.

Jenny: "I think it's trying to tell us about its family or territory. It sounds like it's trying to convey a sense of protectiveness."

Lisa: "I agree. It's trying to communicate something about its home or its community."

Tom: "I think it's trying to tell us that it's threatened and wants us to understand and respect its presence in the forest." Then it came through loud and clear. "You leave my home and go to your home. Humans kill our food and take it away. They destroy our home. Do not tell humans where you found us. We want to be alone in our home." The group froze in awe as a towering figure stepped out of the forest. It was a female Sasquatch, unlike anything they had ever seen before.

But as they watched, they continued hearing her voice in their minds, a message sent telepathically from the creature. She spoke of peace, the importance of preserving the natural world, and the need for humans not to look and find them. Humans will hunt and kill our children. They will kill us and our food.

The group felt sad about what the female Sasquatch had just conveyed. Lisa said, " we need to honor their wishes and not give out this location. People will flock to this area and hunt or kill them."

The group had been communicating with the female Sasquatch for some time. The Sasquatch's thoughts transfixed them, their hearts swelling with a sense of connection to the natural world. When the message was finished, both Sasquatch turned and disappeared back into the forest, leaving them with a sense of wonder and a renewed commitment to preserving the fragile beauty of the world around them.

Tom: "It looks like they're moving away from us. It's like they're disappearing into the forest."

Jenny: "Yeah, it's almost like they've said what they needed to say, and now they're leaving. We need to distance ourselves too."

Lisa: "I wish we could follow them and continue to communicate. It's such a unique opportunity to learn more about these creatures."

Skyler: "Yeah, but we have to respect their need for privacy and space. They've shown us they're intelligent and capable of communication; we should be grateful for that."

The group's encounter with the Sasquatch was a thrilling and a unique experience, but it left them questioning the true meaning of the Sasquatch existence. At first, they believed they couldn't understand and convey specific messages. Still, upon further reflection, they realized the communication was far more complex and nuanced than they had initially thought.

Despite their attempts to understand at first, the group recognized that they were likely interpreting the Sasquatch's sounds and tones through their human perspective, which may have limited their ability to fully grasp the true meaning behind the telepathy. They realized the Sasquatch's communication had expressed the protectiveness of family, territory, and food supply.

Although the group was disappointed they could not communicate more effectively with the Sasquatch, they still felt a sense of wonder and amazement at the experience. They realized that the Sasquatch were intentionally communicating with them, and this encounter gave them a glimpse into these elusive creatures' mysterious world.

After the Sasquatch had moved away from them and disappeared into the forest, the group proceeded to the base camp and set up for the night. They sat around the fire, talking about the communication with the Sasquatch. With the telepathic thoughts they had heard, they understood what the Sasquatch had been trying to say. They couldn't help but feel a sense of disappointment that they had not been able to communicate with the Sasquatch at first, but they knew that the experience had given them a glimpse into the mysterious world of these creatures.

The group couldn't help but feel a sense of ease as the night grew darker. They knew they were alone in the wilderness and many unknowns were lurking in the forest. Despite the fear, Jenny sensed that they were finally not going to see Sasquatch in the wilderness anymore. They were in awe of the natural beauty of the forest and the creatures that called it home.

As the night ended, the group knew they would be safe for the night and then leave the area in the morning. They had reached the end of their journey, and it was time to return home. They were tired from the hike and the excitement of the day.

The next morning the group packed their tents and sleeping bags and hiked out of the forest and to their vehicles.

They drove to Skyler's' home, went inside and sat at his table. Skyler made a pot of coffee to help calm their nerves. Then they wrote their notes and compared them to each other; they all had very similar accounts. Lisa compiled all the evidence, the photos, the audio and video, the hair samples and footprint casts. There was ample proof of Sasquatch to submit to UBC, and the community at large. Dr. Ross agreed that the location would be kept secret out of respect for Sasquatch. She knew that humans would hunt and kill them for their sense of glory.

Jenny and Skyler disappeared briefly to discuss their time together and the subsequent progression of their relationship. They had only met a few days ago, but they had grown very close then. Jenny and Skyler embraced and held each other tightly, not wanting to let go, exchanging loving kisses and talking about him flying to Vancouver in a week to see her. Jenny started to cry, and he held her even more tightly, telling her she was safe and would be forever now that they were together. She said goodbye to him and that she loved him. He said that he loved her too. Then she told Lisa and Tom she was ready to go. Still, tears were visibly running down her cheeks. They got into Tom's truck and said their goodbyes to Skyler. Skyler waved as they drove off back to Terrace.

As Tom drove Jenny and Dr. Lisa back to the Rosswood General Store, the tension in the car was palpable. The three of them were still in shock after encountering the Sasquatch, and they were all coming to terms with what had happened. When they arrived at the store, they immediately told the owner about their experience. He listened intently, nodding his head as they described the Sasquatch and their close encounter with the creature. "I am glad you got out alive," he said, his voice filled with concern. "The wilderness can be dangerous, and you never know what you might come across."

Tom, Jenny, and Dr. Ross agreed. They were grateful to have made it out of the forest alive, and they were able to capture the evidence of Sasquatch's existence. They had discovered proof of the creature's existence, but their encounter had been too brief, especially after meeting the female Sasquatch and what she had said to them.

After speaking with the store owner, the trio returned to the Terrace Airport for their flight back to Vancouver. As they drove, they reflected on their experience in the wilderness and what it meant for their research. They were determined to continue their research for Sasquatch and were

...ing their next expedition.

...y arrived at the airport, they said their goodbyes and boarded ... back to Vancouver. The flight was quiet. Lisa and Jenny spent most of the time lost thinking about the Sasquatch and their encounter in the forest. As they landed in Vancouver, they felt a sense of relief wash over them. They were back in civilization, where things felt safe and familiar. They collected their belongings and headed to the airport exit, where they would catch a taxi to their homes.

Jenny was the first to arrive at her apartment. She felt exhausted and drained, but she knew she needed to tell her roommate what had happened. When she opened the door and placed her backpack and equipment on the floor, her roommate rushed to her, asking what was wrong. Jenny tried to explain what had happened but broke down in tears, unable to find the words to describe what she had gone through and seen. She told her about meeting the man of her dreams, Skyler and their plans for the future.

Dr. Lisa arrived at her home a short time later. She was greeted by her husband David, who had seen and heard the news on the TV news station and was worried. Dr. Lisa hugged her husband tightly, grateful for his support finally. She explained what had happened in the forest, and her husband listened intently, not interrupting her once.

Once they had settled in and rested, Lisa started receiving calls from their colleagues and friends in the scientific community. Everyone wanted to know what had happened and what they had seen. She called Jenny about the phone calls she received, and Jenny said her phone was blowing up from calls too.

The next day, they made their way back to their research lab at the University of British Columbia, where they would analyze their data and plan their next steps. UBC told them they needed to release this evidence to the world, and they both agreed with UBC to hold a press conference to share their findings with the world.

As they worked, they were filled with a sense of determination and excitement. They had definitive proof of Sasquatch's existence and were determined to continue their research with more solid evidence of Sasquatch's existence. They were grateful for their collected evidence and eager to share their findings with the world.

Despite their challenges in the wilderness, they remained optimistic and driven. They knew that their research was essential and determined to see it through to the end. They were grateful for the support they had received from their colleagues, and they were inspired by the incredible community of Sasquatch researchers who had come before them.

Dr. Lisa Ross finally presented her findings to the scientific community. She had been working on her report for the past week and was eager to share her findings with the world. Her team's discovery of Sasquatch in the Nass Valley had been a major breakthrough in the world of anthropology, and she was excited to be a part of it.

The report was based on the hair samples collected from the Sasquatch, the foot castings, pictures, videos, and audio evidence. The hair samples were analyzed in a laboratory, and the results were conclusive. The DNA analysis showed that the creature was a new hominid species not previously known to science.

Dr. Ross gave a presentation at the University of British Columbia, outlining her findings and the evidence collected. The presentation was well received, and many of the audience members were impressed by the quality of the evidence. The pictures, videos, and audio recordings were especially compelling, and many people in the audience were amazed by what they saw and heard.

The report was also well received by the scientific community at large. Dr. Ross's team was credited with significantly contributing to the field of anthropology, and the report was widely discussed in scientific journals and magazines.

Dr. Ross and her team also received recognition from the Nisga'a

Nation communities in the Nass Valley. The communities were grateful for the team's respect for their land and understanding of Sasquatch's importance to their culture and traditions.

Jenny, Tom, and Officer Skyler Kane were also acknowledged in the report for their contributions to the team's success. Jenny was recognized for her tireless search for Sasquatch, and Tom was acknowledged for his tracking skills and expertise in wilderness survival. Officer Kane was recognized for his knowledge of the Nass Valley, his wilderness survival skills, and his protection and support of the team.

The report was a major triumph for Dr. Ross, Jenny and her team, and they were proud of their achievements. They had made a significant contribution to the field of anthropology and had shed new light on the existence of Sasquatch.

Major news outlets covered the report, and several media outlets interviewed Dr. Ross, including CNN and the National Geographic Channel. She was able to share her findings and her team's experiences with the world, and her team finally received the recognition they deserved.

The report was also a turning point for Sasquatch research. It helped to legitimize the search for Sasquatch and encouraged other researchers to take the field more seriously. The report was widely cited in other scientific studies and helped lay the foundation for future Sasquatch research.

In conclusion, Dr. Lisa Ross's report on the positive finding of Sasquatch in the Nass Valley was a major milestone in the field of anthropology. Her team's discovery was a significant contribution to the scientific community, and they were recognized for their achievements. The report helped to shed new light on the existence of Sasquatch and was a turning point for Sasquatch research.

The press conference was held in a large conference room at the University of British Columbia. There were reporters and photographers from all over the world, and the room was filled with excitement and anticipation.

Dr. Ross, Jenny, Tom and Skyler took to the stage and spoke about their experience in the forest. They showed the footage they had captured on the Kermode bears and explained the evidence they had found on Sasquatch. Jenny spoke about being taken by a ten-foot male Sasquatch to a cave and told not to let humans destroy the forest, food and their existence. The room was silent as she spoke, and her words captivated the audience. Tom told the audience of the great white light that enveloped him. Jenny and Lisa witnessed this light that took him up and out of their site, only to be returned 10 hours later that night. Skyler spoke about what the female Sasquatch had telepathically told them about needing their location held in secret. She did not want humans destroying the forest, their food, and the Sasquatch to be hunted and killed.

After the press conference, they were flooded with offers from television shows, documentaries, and magazines. They were in high demand and soon found themselves being interviewed on national and international news programs.

Their research became a sensation and the face of Sasquatch research. People were fascinated by their stories, and they were soon recognized as experts in the field. They continued to study Sasquatch and other mysterious creatures, and their findings continued to make waves in the scientific community.

Their findings and research changed how people thought about Sasquatch, and they are now remembered as the scientists who helped shed light on one of the world's greatest mystery. They continued to work together, building on their findings and making discoveries, and they remained friends and colleagues for the rest of their lives.

Betterment of the world

Dr. Lisa Ross, Tom Miller, and a team of five UBC scientists convened to discuss cutting-edge space age technology that could further advance the human race. Their primary objectives were to end world hunger and to create a free and renewable source of energy, new technology to usher in the new space age human, and new medical breakthroughs.

Dr. Lisa Ross and Tom Miller, along with a team of scientists, successfully developed a revolutionary new food source that changed the way food was produced. This innovation quickly gained global attention, and factories were built worldwide to produce this new food source.

The scientists utilized advanced genetic engineering techniques to create a highly efficient, nutrient-rich food source that could be grown quickly and sustainably. This new food source could be cultivated in large quantities in controlled environments, using minimal resources and land.

The factories that produced this new food source quickly became popular worldwide, as they offered a sustainable solution to the global hunger crisis. With the world's population growing at an unprecedented rate, the new food source offered a scalable solution that could feed the masses without depleting the planet's natural resources.

The success of this new food source revolutionized the food production industry, with more and more factories being built worldwide to meet the increasing demand. The once pressing issue of world hunger was now no longer a problem, thanks to the innovation of Dr. Lisa Ross, Tom Miller, and their team of scientists.

This breakthrough in food production not only fed the world's population but also created new economic opportunities and improved the quality of life for many communities worldwide. The legacy of this invention continued to inspire new generations of scientists and innovators to push the boundaries of what is possible and make the world a better place.

Tom showcased the necessary resources for mass production of energy, all sourced from asteroids. The team of scientists built prototypes in Vancouver, using these asteroid-mined elements to power the UBC campus and its buildings.

The team collaborated with engineers and technicians to ensure the energy systems were reliable and efficient. They developed an advanced monitoring system to keep track of energy production and usage, making adjustments to optimize performance.

Finally, after months of testing and hard work, the free and renewable energy system, powered entirely by elements mined from asteroids, was launched. The UBC campus and its buildings were successfully powered by this space-age technology, significantly reducing their carbon footprint and energy bills.

The success of this project inspired other communities and institutions to explore space-mined elements as a viable source of renewable energy. The team led by Dr. Lisa Ross and Tom Miller continued to innovate and develop new technologies, pushing the boundaries of what was possible with space-age technology.

A new era of space travel was ushered in as Dr. Lisa Ross, Tom Miller, and the team of scientists developed revolutionary space-age ships that could leave Earth without the need for rocket fuel. This new propulsion technology enabled spaceships to cruise to Mars in just three days, opening up access to other galaxies that were once beyond reach.

The team also developed a new method of asteroid mining that brought in the necessary elements for ship protection and building structures on other planets. This breakthrough enabled the construction of advanced and sustainable space stations on other planets, with the potential to support human life.

With these advancements, space travel became more efficient, reliable, and sustainable than ever before. The new space-age ships were equipped with state-of-the-art technology that ensured safe and comfortable travel for the crew. The ships were also designed to be more environmentally friendly, with minimal emissions and waste.

As more and more people ventured into space, new opportunities for exploration, and resource acquisition emerged. The team led by Dr. Lisa Ross and Tom Miller continued to push the boundaries of space technology, inspiring new generations of scientists and innovators to explore and expand the frontiers of space.

In summary, the development of space-age ships and asteroid mining technology revolutionized space travel, making it more accessible, sustainable, and efficient. With these advancements, humanity could now explore new frontiers and other planets and unlock the universe's secrets.

Dr. Lisa Ross, Jenny, Tom Miller, Skyler Kane, and a team of scientists revolutionized the medical field with breakthrough advancements that ushered in the cure for all diseases. This groundbreaking achievement led to an unprecedented increase in life expectancy, as people no longer had to suffer from debilitating illnesses that once shortened their lifespans.

Moreover, the team also developed brain implants that could enhance brain capacity to 100% usage, effectively unlocking the full potential of the human brain. With these implants, humans achieved higher levels of cognitive function, leading to increased intelligence, memory, and creativity.

As a result of these advancements, humanity achieved a higher level of power, with the ability to communicate through telepathy. This breakthrough in communication allowed people to share their thoughts, ideas, and emotions instantaneously, revolutionizing the way humans interacted with each other.

The team's achievements in the medical field and neuroscience opened up new possibilities for humanity, with the potential for further advancements in space travel, engineering, and artificial intelligence. With longer life expectancy and increased cognitive function, people could now pursue more important and ambitious goals that were once thought impossible.

The legacy of Dr. Lisa Ross, Jenny, Tom Miller, Skyler Kane, and their team of scientists continued to inspire new generations of scientists and innovators to push the boundaries of what is possible in the medical field and beyond. They paved the way for a brighter and more prosperous future for humanity, where the limits of the human mind and body were yet to be fully realized.

The Proposal

Jenny and Skyler kept in touch through long-distance communication as Jenny was busy completing her Ph.D. Despite the distance, they both knew that their relationship was strong, and they were committed to making it work. They would talk on the phone daily, sending each other emails and pictures, and Skyler would visit Jenny whenever he could.

During that time, Jenny worked hard on her research and finally completed her Ph.D. She was proud of her accomplishment and couldn't wait to share the news with Skyler. Dr. Lisa Ross attended her graduation. Skyler, and Tom flew down for the Graduation. They both attended the dance and continued the celebration. When she finally saw him in person, they hugged each other tightly and celebrated with a romantic dinner.

After that, they decided to move in together, both ready to take the next step in their relationship. They found a cozy apartment in the city and settled into a routine, spending most of their free time exploring and travelling together.

Jenny was happy to have Skyler by her side, and he was happy to be with her. They both knew that they had found something special in each other and were determined to make it last.

One day, while walking along the beach, Skyler knelt down on one knee and proposed to Jenny. She was overjoyed, and of course, she said yes. They hugged and kissed, and then Skyler placed the ring on Jenny's finger.

Their wedding was a beautiful ceremony, with friends and family in attendance. They exchanged vows in front of the stunning ocean and promised to love and cherish each other for the rest of their lives.

After the wedding, they went on a romantic honeymoon to a tropical island, where they spent their days lounging on the beach and exploring the lush tropical forests.

Jenny and Skyler were thrilled together and looking forward to a bright future together. They were both grateful for the journey that had brought them together and was looking forward to the many adventures still coming in the NASS Valley.

They never forgot about their encounter with the Male and Female Sasquatch in the Nass Valley.

The Research Community

The Sasquatch community has been around for over 100 years. Over the past century, numerous sightings, encounters, and alleged evidence have been reported, fueling the public's fascination with Sasquatch.

While some skeptics dismiss Sasquatch as a myth or legend, others believe that there is enough evidence to suggest that this creature may indeed exist.

Today, the Sasquatch community is more active than ever, with individuals and organizations dedicated to researching and investigating reported sightings and evidence. The use of advanced technology, such as drones and thermal imaging, has also enabled researchers to explore remote areas and gather new evidence.

In addition to scientific research, the Sasquatch community has also inspired a vibrant culture of art, literature, and entertainment. Numerous books, films, and TV shows have been produced that explore the myths, legends, and potential existence of Sasquatch, further fueling public fascination with this creature.

The Sasquatch community has also had a significant impact on local economies, with many areas promoting Sasquatch tourism and merchandise sales. From museums and festivals to guided tours and souvenirs, Sasquatch has become a lucrative business for many communities.

There have been many individuals who have dedicated their time and efforts to researching Sasquatch over the years. Here are some notable names of Sasquatch researchers, both past, and present:

1. Rene Dahinden - A Canadian Sasquatch researcher who dedicated over 40 years of his life to researching and investigating Sasquatch sightings and evidence.
2. Peter Byrne - An Irish-born Sasquatch researcher who founded the Sasquatch Information Center and Exhibition in Oregon, USA, in the 1970s.
3. Grover Krantz - An American anthropologist who conducted extensive research on Sasquatch footprints and argued that the creature may be a surviving member of the Gigantopithecus genus.
4. Dr. Jeff Meldrum - An American professor of anatomy and anthropology who has conducted extensive research on Sasquatch footprints and morphology and written several books on the subject.
5. Cliff Barackman - A Sasquatch researcher and co-host of the Animal Planet show "Finding Sasquatch," who has conducted numerous investigations and expeditions in search of Sasquatch.
6. Dr. John Bindernagel - A Canadian wildlife biologist who has written several books on the subject of Sasquatch and conducted field research in areas known for Sasquatch sightings.
7. Todd Standing - A Sasquatch researcher who has filmed Sasquatch on multiple occasions and produced several documentaries on the subject.

These are just a few of the many researchers who have dedicated their time and efforts to studying Sasquatch over the years. While opinions and approaches may vary, their work has contributed to the ongoing discussion and fascination with this elusive creature.

About the Author

John MacLellan is a talented author and musician who hails from Cape Breton, Nova Scotia, but has made Terrace, British Columbia his home for the past 36 years. Throughout his time in Terrace, John has developed a deep respect for the local cultures and has immersed himself in the community.

In addition to his love of writing, John is also an accomplished guitarist and has played in several local bands, including Grey Wolf, Crooked String, and Bad Reputation. He has recorded with Brad Heartly and Ryan Krumm known as Big Skinny. Big Skinny had their music played on CFNR radio. Lynn Turbasket also interviewed Brad and John on the radio. His musical talents have brought him great joy and have allowed him to connect with others in the community.

More recently, John has taken to writing and has become an accomplished author. With NASS VALLEY SASQUATCH, John draws on his extensive knowledge of the wilderness to create a thrilling tale of adventure and discovery. His fascination with Sasquatch legends and sightings led him to research the topic extensively, and his book is a testament to his dedication and love for the natural world.

Whether you are a fan of adventure stories, a lover of Sasquatch lore, or simply someone who enjoys a good mystery, John's book is a must-read. With its vivid descriptions of the rugged landscape and its unforgettable cast of characters, NASS VALLEY SASQUATCH is sure to captivate and enthrall readers from start to finish.

Manufactured by Amazon.ca
Bolton, ON